LAALI MERE LAAL KI.

Definition of friendship.

Rishab K.

pencil

ISBN 978-93-5667-392-2

Published in India 2023 by Pencil

A brand of
One Point Six Technologies Pvt. Ltd.
123, Building J2, Shram Seva Premises,
Wadala Truck Terminal, Wadala (E)
Mumbai 400037, Maharashtra, INDIA
E connect@thepencilapp.com
W www.thepencilapp.com

Author biography

Author of this book is a very enthusiastic, determined and dedicated hustling writer who always wants to write something better for the audience. Author Mr. Rishab has won several awards and rewards including district and state awards for writing. He is good in novel, scripts and stories. He is trained professional script writer in Bollywood who has worked with secera production as ghost writer and content developer as well as worked under some very renowned bollywood author.

CONTENTS

Full script.

1 INT/ext. hospital, STADIUM - Day 1

BLACK SCREEN - sounds of a crowd cheering for runners.

QUICK MONTAGE - INTERCUT

- A blurred image of a crowd cheering.
- Bablu (face not visible) runs out of the room and calls out for the doctor.
- Heartbeat sound is heard at a low volume.
- Referee blows a whistle to signal racers to take their place.
- Many runners are kneeling on the race line. Multiple shots of the runners.
- Heartbeat sound is now louder than before.
- A gun shot is heard.
- The runners run and as one of them leaves the start line, dust flies onto the screen.

MOVIE TITLE is displayed.

fade to:

2 Ext. GAGAN'S HOUSE - Night 2

MONTAGE:

- Bike lights directly hits the camera.
- Mukesh is driving the bike along with Bablu.
- A bike stops and the headlight turns off.
- Gagan jumps in front of camera and sits on the bike, and the three of them leave.

2A Ext. ROAD - Night 2A

Montage shots of the road while they are riding a bike.

2B Ext. liquor shop - Night 2B

- BABLU (in his early 20s) goes to the liquor store and buys alcohol in the midst of a small crowd.
- 3 men in their early 20s, including Bablu (other's faces are not visible) are seated and enjoying alcohol.

MONTAGE ENDS

2C Ext. Stage - Night 2C

ITEM SONG as per choreography.

2D Ext. Bus stop - Night 2D

Gagan, Bablu & Mukesh are standing near a road peeing and singing the same song. Bablu tells his friends that he wants to meet Sweety & Gagan decides to help him and so they leave.

3 ext. Sweety's house - Night 3

Bablu climbs up a pole to the first floor of a row house and enters through the window. He goes into the bedroom and sees someone sleeping under a bed-sheet. He walks slowly towards the bed and then jumps towards it, hoping for it to be Sweety.

A man who was sleeping under the sheets gets up angrily and catches Bablu. He turns out to be Sweety's brother and slaps Bablu, but Bablu gets free from his hold and rushes towards the window.

Bablu jumps and falls down, but runs somehow away while Sweety's brother is shouting from the window.

Limping and walking, Bablu reaches a bus stop and takes a break where Gagan and Mukesh reach and find out what happened. They make fun of him and they all laugh together as the night fades into black.

4 Ext. Bittu'S PAAN SHOP - Day 4

QUICK MONTAGE

We see the beauty of Varanasi from a bird's eye point of view. Down below on the streets, several people are working, a sweeper is cleaning the street. A few old people are playing cards.

Bablu is with the old people.

Bablu

Chacha furfura ke apna chaldo,

(kissing his fingers)

humare na haath me aaj khujli mach raha hai.

Old Man

Ama bhatija ho tum moholla ke, bakarpanti utna hi karo jetna chale, e lo humari begum.

old man 2

(laughs out loud)

budhauti me begum rakh ke bhi kono asar naahi hone wala hai, tumhare begum ko le gaya humara badshah.

Bittu

Tum sab ka fir suru ho gaya bhore-bhore, ketna baar kahe hai dhandha ke time me apna adda kahi auro jamao.

Bablu

Ae bittu bhaiya tumhare jo grahak hai na, le de ke yahi sab hai samjhe, ta apna e jo buiness structure hai na esko apne paas rakho.

Mukesh comes to the shop to deliver Gutkha, he has a bag tied up to his cycle from which he hands over the packets to Bittu Paanwala.

MUKESH

Kahe faltu ka khisiya rahe ho bittu bhaiya, jante ho jab sala juu nahi renge ga kisi ke kaan mein bekar apna energy waste kar rahe ho.

Mukesh takes out several pouches of gutkha from his cycle and gives it to Bittu paanwala. Gagan also arrives and greets Mukesh.

Gagan

Ahaa e laye tum kaam ka cheez bey, fresh lali, sala jab tak khae na pressure dhang se nahi ban pata hai.

Mukesh

Pura hindustaan ka same samasya hai, aur hum jaise log samasya ka samadhan, samjhe bittu babu.

Dhanda ka time hai jaldi se dharo hum chale bhaiya.

Gagan looks at Bittu.

Gagan

Pudiya khane wala log na bada sanskari hota hai, ek dam shaant, tab tak kuch nahi bolta hai jab tak pudiya thukk na de…

Bablu

(laughs)

Sahi kaha bhaiwa… I agree bro…

They take the packet and join Bablu who is collecting the money as he gets up.

Mukesh

Kahe fokat mein chacha sabko lapet raho ho haa… saala kaam dhandha karo.

Bablu

humara kamane ka e tarika hai, a tumahara oo… dhandha dhanda hota hai, bhai.

(looks at Bittu)

Bittu bhaiya, edhar bhi lao… humara luck favour mein hai aaj pura udhar clear karega apna Mukesh…

Gagan laughs and Mukesh reacts to Bablu. Bablu gives a packet to Mukesh and has one for himself. They both have the gutkha, and while Gagan is mixing the tobacco someone runs past him, pushing him. The gutkha packet in his hand falls down.

Mukesh and Bablu stand up and a woman shouts from behind them.

Woman

Are kambakat, chor uchakka, sharam nahi aata ek aurat ka bag lekar bhaag raah hai…

Gagan is angry as his gutkha packet fell down and hence runs behind the thief.

Mukesh

Aisa aadmi do hi baar bhaagta hai. Olympic ka race ho ya phir police ka case ho.

Bablu

Aur Gagan ke case mein, jab pudiya waste ho.

5 ext. streets - day 5

Gagan running through the streets and the thief in front of him. The thief changes streets and Gagan follows. Gagan takes a shortcut and reaches in front of the thief.

Gagan

Bete Gagan naam hai humara, humare nazar se door kaha bhaag paoge. Jao tumko option dete hai iss gali mein pakade ya agla mein.

The thief continues to run even faster. Gagan keeps chasing him and finally catches him.Gagan catches the thief by the collar.

thief

Ae bhaiyaa ruk jao 2 sec haaf gaye hai hum… bhaiya tumhara kya bigade hai… maa kasam ab se kono purse nahi nochenge…

Gagan

Kasam gaya tel lene. pehle e batao pudiya kahe giraya humara?

Thief

Hein… kon pudiya… acha ta tum humare peecha uske liye kiye… bade bagairat ho yaar tum… aise thodi hota hai… hum jaa rahe hai.

Gagan

Abey ruko… ek to humara nuksaan upar se tumhara e swabhimaan…

nikale jaldi kya hai jeb mein…

Gagan checking the pockets of the thief as he struggles.

Thief

pura le lo ge kya? humara bhi baal bacha hai guru…

Gagan

E humara pudiya ka bharpayi, aur e humare daudne ka….

Gagan takes all the money from the thief's pocket along with a packet of Gutkha from him.

Thief

Bhaiya, bhut door ghar se samjho guru… kam se kam bhaada to chodo.

Gagan

Tum bhaagta acha ho, jao bhaago…

As the thief is about to leave, Gagan remembers something and stops him.

Gagan

Abey purse idhar lao.

Gagan pushes the thief and walks away.

6 Ext. Bittu'S PAAN SHOP - Day 6

Mukesh and Bablu are talking about Gagan, when a rickshaw arrives and Gagan gets down.

Gagan goes towards the woman who is still standing there.

Woman

Are bhut badhiya Beta… khub naam kamao…… bhgwaan tumhare jaisa beta sab ko de…

Gagan

chachi aashirvaad to dete rehna… pehle ek kaam karo riksha wala ka bhada de do….

She mutters something a bit angrily and Gagan walks towards his friends.

Bablu

Tum to yaar dhavak nikle bey?

Mukesh

Olympics mein kahe nahe try karte ho

Gagan

Abey ee sab latihad cheezein hain, zindagi ek hi baar mila hai sala esko aise waste thodi karna hai….

(eats gutkha)

Humri planning toh kuch aur hai.

Mukesh's brother comes running and calls out to Gagan.

chhotu

ladoo bhaiya jaldi ghar jaiye, Sumitra mausi phirse pagla gayi hai pata nahi kya-kya bole jaa rahi hai…

Gagan

Arre yaar mummy…

Gagan leaves in a hurry.

7 Ext. GAGAN'S HOUSE (VERANDA) - Day 7

Gagan reaches his home and spits the tobacco outside the house at the spot where 2 kids are seated sucking lollipop. Gagan asks the kid with hand signs as to what is going on in his house. The kids look at each other and laugh and run away.

7A INT. GAGAN'S HOUSE (HALL) - Day 7A

Sumitraji is piercing the nose of a local girl using a pin or similar instrument.

chanda

Jaan maar dogi kya sumitra chachi… halka haath se karo na…

Sumitra Devi

Humko na sikhao... aadha mohalla ka naak kaan humi chedhe hai… aur to koi tumhare tarah natak nahi kiya.

Chanda

Hum thode hi sabka theka liye hue hai, hum apna dekhenge ki mohalla ka…

Sumitra Devi

Mudi seedha karo, aur ek dam chup chap se baetho 2 min lagega… humko….

Chanda screams out loud.

Gagan

Are mummy kya kar rahi ho tum aaram se…

Chanda

ek dam hi nishtur ho tum… sach bataye rahe hai… sabka mat mara gaya jo tumse karwane aati hai…

Sumitra Devi

Are jao-jao… badi aayi… jana kahi aur, itna kam mein pura banaras mein koi kar diya na… toh hum bhi dekhte hai…

Gagan

kya hua mummy kahe subah-subah khisiyae rahi ho…

Sumitra Devi

Tum toh beta bolo hi mat, humrae zindagi mein tum baap beta thaan liye ho ki khusi nahi aane doge, aisa kya julum kar diye aakhir hum…

GAGAN

Fir chalu ho gaya tumhara…. sab dukh bhagwan kya tumhai ko diye hai.

Sumitra Devi

(picks up some things)

Aisa kya galat bole hum, ek to tmhare papa humesa alage mijaj mein rehte hai unko toh kuch bolna hi paap hai, upar se tum bhi aise hi nikal gaye… hum kare to kare kya…

Gagan

Tum kya chahti ho, hum kya kare?

Sumitra Devi

Sachi batae…

Gagan

(waiting for his mom's answer)

batao…

Sumitraji comes and sits near Gagan.

Sumitra Devi

Hum kya bol rahe hai beta suno 24 ka umra ho gaya hai tumhara… kab tak humare pallu ko pakad ke ghumoge … ek bhute acha rishta hai, yahi banars mein… apana hi caste hai…

(Shying a bit)

samdhi ji ka kapda ka dukaan hai wo bhi ladies wear.

Gagan

(murmuring)

Samdhi ji

Sumitra Devi

ek dam badhiya rishta hai tum bas ek baar chal lo humare saath…

Gagan gets up and sits on the cot near where Dadaji is sleeping.

Gagan

Mummy hum tumko kitna baar bole hai… ki abhi nahi karna shaadi humko yaar abhi hum khali 24 ke hue hai… Daadu aap hi samjahiye amma ko…

Sumitra Devi

Beta to dikkat kya hai ek baar shaadi kar lo fir karte rahna jo karna hai tumko… koi pressure thode hai…

Gagan

Mummy abhi bahut kuch hai life mein…… tum kaise samjhaye hum…

Daddu… Daddu…

There is a brief moment of silence, as if Gagan's grandfather passed away. Sumitraji and Gagan come closer to dadaji, since he is not responding.

Gagan

Daadu daadu…

Gagan picks up the bed sheet from one side in fear and sees dadaji's feet. Dadaji gets up from the opposite side.

DADAJI

Kahe itna chillam chilli macha rakhe ho dono maa beta… Bhuchad khane me bhi kum se kum esse jyada shanti rehta hai.

Sumitra Devi

(makes a face)

Toh wahi chale jaiye naa…

(murmuring to herself)

yaha kon sa koi rok raha hai.

Gagan

Daddu aap bhi mummy ko samajhiye, ee koi umar hai shaadi karne ka…

Dadaji

Hum ek baar pradhanmantri ko kuch samjha sakte hai lekin esko samjhana, bael ke saamne hara jhandi dikhana hai.

Sumitra Devi

Lekin bael to laal rang se bhadakti hai naa…

Dadaji

Toh hum lal rang kaha pehne hai jo humare peeche padi ho…

Sumitra Devi

(thinking)

Hum nahi jaante, tum humare saath chalo kal… ladki samjh mein aa gayi to theek hai nahi to fir tum jaisa bolo hum waisa karenge… aap hi samjhaiye…

Dadaji

Hum ka smjhaye Hum jabardasti toh iski shadi nahi kara sakata. Jab karna hoga kar lega.

Sumitra Devi

Thik hai hum hi keh dete hai. Beta hum na marne ka soch liya hain. Market se tanik jeher leke aa aana.

Gagan

Maa kahe nautanki kar rahi ho?

Dadaji laughs out loud.

Sumitra Devi

Hum nautanki kar rahe hain? Dekho jara humari taraf humara mann nahi karta beta ka shaadi dekhe.

Gagan walks away from his mother and towards his grandfather.

Gagan

Maa hum shaddi toh nahi karenge,kum se kum abhi toh nahi aur arrange marriage to ek dam nahi.

Ee humri umar hai shaadi karne ki? Daddu…

Dadaji

Beta tumhari umar me tumhara baap humre godh me tha.

Sumitra Devi

Aur ee ka fashion bata rahe ho arrange marriage nahi karna hai?

Dekho humne ladki dekh li hai. Ab tum dekh lo aur pasand kar lo hum kal subah jaa rahe hai. Ladki pasand aa jaaye to do-chaar baar banaras ghuma dena usko.

Tumhara love marriage ka thasak bhi pura ho jayega.

Sumitra devi leaves while Gagan waits back speechless.

8 Int. BRIJNANDAN RAM'S HOUSE - Day
8

Gagan and his parents are seated on a sofa along with Brijnandan Ram and Kausalya devi (Suman's parents).

There is an odd silence among them and the sound of water dripping from the roof outside is heard.

Murariji and his wife both take one each. Sumitraji gives them a plastic bag full of papad.

MURARI JI

(while eating a samosa)

Samosa bada gazab ka hai bhabhi ji, Madhuri ki yaad aa gayi wo bhi aise hi samose banati thi…

Sumitra coughs and looks at her husband. Murariji feels a bit awkward and hence concentrates on the samosa.

Kausalya

Bhabhiji aap bhi lijie na samosa…

Gagan smiles with his mouth close and shows his hand to signal a no.

Murari Ji

Baarish toh nahi hai ho rahi, toh yeh paani tapakne ka awaaz kahan se aa raha hai?

Kausalya looks at her husband Brijnandan.

Brijnandan

(looks at Kaushalya)

Tanki mein ched ho rakha hai, lalu ko boli nahi tum…

He takes a pause and then looks at Gagan.

Brijnandan

Toh beta aap kya kaam karte hai?

Murari Ji
Sidha mudde par aa gaya
(muttering)
ahmm…
(looks at Sumitra)
tum batayi nahi… humara naav hai khud ka…
Sumitra Devi
Bataye the naa… humara apna naav hai… humara Gagan hi sab sambhalta hai… ab es umra mein itna kaam kon kare… bahut honhaar aur mehnati hai humara bitwa. Inka toh tension hi khatam kar diya sara.
Kausalya
Acha ji bahut badhiya, ladka aise hi hona chahiye. Sach kahe to hum aise hi saadha ladka dhoondh rahe thhe Suman ke liye.
Brijnandan
Bas humara ek hi manna tha ladka ko koi kharab aadat na ho,
Gagan's parents freeze and look towards Gagan.
Murari Ji
Are nai-nai humara beta toh gau hai gau. Koi bhi nasha nahi karta.
Brijnandan
Tab toh aur koi baat hi nahi reh gaya. Ladka kamata hai, sanskari hai, isse badhiya rishta humko kya chahie…
Hum toh isliye pareshan ho raha tha. Aaj kal ka jo estithi hai bahut kharab hai.
Yahi humare bagal me ek Jugnu karke ladka hai. Din bhar pudiya, bidi aur naake par baaith kar jua khelna. Ek din Suman ka hanth mangane chala aaya.
Gagan's parents move a bit further in curiosity. Sound of the water dripping a bit prominent due to the silence.

Sumitra Devi
Phir?
Brijnandan
Phir kya, hum bhi desi darzi hai esi silaayi machine me ungli cheep diye…
Kausalya
Ab aise logo ko kaun apni beti deta bhala…
Gagan's parents look at each other a bit nervously.
Brijnandan
Tum bhi kya baat karne lag gai. Suman ko bulao.
Kausalya
Abhi leke aate hai.
Brijnandan
Murari ji beti ko humne sanskar ke alava kuch diye hi nahi hai, eska shaadi karke humara bhi mann hai Kuch haridwar chal jaye…
Suman ke dada dadi wahi rahte hai… wahi par kuch din acha se bitayenge…
Baaki ladki jo hai humari ek dam sundar, sushil aur sewa karne wali hai…
There is a sudden sound of something falling in the kitchen, and they all look towards the kitchen. The sound of the water dropping is now more prominent.
Brijnandan
Lagta hai billi hogi sayad…
Murari Ji
Badi wali Billi … kahi kaali Billi to nahi… zara dekhiye
Murariji looks at Gagan and Sumitra. Brijnandan Ram gets up to welcome his daughter.
Brijnandan
Lo aa gayi humri Suman.

Suman comes in with tea and Gagan looks up to see her face. Suman is wearing makeup & has large teeth that are visible. Gagan is in shock & accidentally laughs out.

Gagan spits out the gutkha in his mouth towards Brijnandan Ram and it stains his entire white shirt. Suman looks horrified to see Gagan.

An awkward silence follows along with the sound of the water dripping constantly as the looks on the faces of Brijnandan and Kausalya say it all.

8A Ext. BRIJNANDAN RAM'S HOUSE (DOOR) - Day 8A

The door is closed with a loud thud.

MURARI JI

Arey samdhi ji humari baat toh suniye…

cut to:

9 Ext. ROAD - Day 9

Murariji, Gagan and Sumitra devi are seated in an e-rickshaw.

MURARI JI

Beta aur kitna naak kataogey baap ka. Kumse kum dusron ke ghar pe toh apna ee sab pan pudiya band karo… hum ta tumko sudhar pae nahi…

(looking towards Sumitra)

Sun rahi ho sumitra kuldrohi ko janni ho tum. Dekhna ek din pura kul ka vinash yahi karega.

GAGAN

Beta aap ke hi to hai… Maa ko kahe tana maar rahe hai? Maa thodi humko google se download ki hai.

SUMITRA DEVI

Shabhaas beta!!

MURARI JI

Tum chup raho! Humare to tum ho hi nahi, confirmed!

SUMITRA DEVI

Nahi to kya? humne committee daali thi isko paida karne ke time pe?

Iske harkate dekh ke toh aisa hi lagta hai ki aap hi ka hai.

GAGAN

Aap log humko daat rahe hai ki aapas me jhagdaa kar rahe hai

Murari Ji

Jawaani toh humari tum ko palne mein gaya, abhi budhapa tumri chinta me jaega.

Beta hum kya kare, bhut chintit hai tumko leke…

Gagan

Mummy tumhare kehne par hum aaye thhe ladki dekhne. Dekha na kya hua

Ab shaadi ke baare me humse koi baat nahi karega, bas!

Murari Ji

Beta waise bhi tumko ladki to koi dene wala hai nahi…

Sumitra Devi

Subh-subh boliye aap… dekhne bhut sundar bahu aaegi es ghar mein…

They reach their house. Bablu and Mukesh also arrive on a bike.

Bablu

Ram-Ram chacha, Ram-Ram chachi. Mithai Khaiye…

Murari Ji

Mithai nahi, pitai ki jarurat hai tum logon ko.

Bablu

Bas kya chacha… itna pyaar kahe?

Mukesh

ladki pasand aayi ki nahi.

Gagan rushes towards the bike and pushes Mukesh to move forward and make place for him to sit.

Gagan

Chal beta bahut ho gaya enquiry.

Mukesh

Ram-ram chachi.

Sumitra Devi

Dhyaan se jaana lalla. Mera lal…

Murari Ji

E khali tumhara lal nahi pure mohalle ka lal hai… eske bas chale na to tajmahal ko bhi thuk-thuk ke lal kila banade….

Sumitra taps Murariji indicating their home has arrived and points towards the door.

10 Ext. Govt. COllege - Day 10

Mukesh, Bablu and Gagan are seated at a tea shop near a girl's college, laughing loudly at Gagan.

Bablu

Tum sala chacha ko lal kar diye…

bhai lekin ek baat batae love is blind…

Mukesh bursts out laughing.

GAGAN

Abey bas karo yaar… Woh toh aise hi time pass tha, ab hum kya karte yaar matalb achanak se humare saamne aayi humse controle nahi hua…

Mukesh

I can understand… bro hum samajhte hai tumhara estithi…

Bablu

dekhiye bol kon raha hai, beta ladki dekhe ho kabhi…

Girlfriend word tumhare aukaat ke bahar hai, uske liye style chahie… samjha.

Paanwala who hears all of them talking laughs out at this.
MUKESH
Hahaha bada hasi aa raha guru tmko, muh me daalo batti aur pudiya khilao… chup chap… bada maza aa raha hai.
Bablu
Acha suno humara baat, bhut gyaan ka baat bata rahe hai…
ladki patane ka upaaye…
Pehla ladki ko kya chahie hota hai ki ladka pura lanth ho… oh bataegi nahi lekin e fact hai…
Mukesh
(smiles)
Bad boys…
Bablu
Dusra jo usko ek dam daab ke rakhe… kaheki unlogo ko pasand hota hai hard ladka…
Ee sab babu, baby khali cinema mein hota hai asli mein aise bolte hai… ae sun rahi ho
Sweety arrives over there and hears Bablu, who notices her.
Bablu
Kaisi ho baby… chalo tumko mast chaat khilate hai,
(whistles and leaves)
kachodi wala thik hai bhai log tum apna dekho hum chale…
Mukesh and Gagan laugh while Bablu leaves in a hurry on his bike.
11 ext. GANGA GHAT - Day 11
A foreigner girl is clicking photos of chillua.
Chillua
(Making a pose)

You like this… This is Banaras ghat… U know Bholenath…

Chillua is busy flirting with a foreigner taking photos.

Krishna Murari reaches the ganga ghat. He washes his hand in the Ganga & search of Chillua when he sees him with the foreigner. Krishna ji pulls Chillua by the ears.

Murari Ji

Tumko kitna baar samjhae hai ki kaam ke time pe e sab chirandu panti karna paap hai… ek toh hum sala apne beta se tabah se upar se tum…

Chillua

(to the foreigner)

Sorry…

(looks at Murariji)

Hekho Murari akele hum tum humko chahe kuch bhi bol lo… angrezo ke saamne koi izzat hai…

Chillua starts to untie one of the boats when Pankaj arrives on another boat.

PANKAJ

Murariji, kya hua bitwa ke lagan ka?

Murari Ji

Arre pehle kutte se aadmi toh ban jae tab na karayenge shaadi?

Chillua

Jawaan khoon hai, samajh jayega, Murari, kahe piche pade hue ho.

Murariji unties and pushes another boat with a little force.

Murari Ji

Pehle to tum hume Murari bolna band karo… tumhare baa kea umar ke hai hum.

Pankaj laughs at Chillua and continues with his work.

Chillua

Izzat jo hai na kamana padta hai, choro tum nahi samjhoge…

Murari Ji

Yahi baandh ke maarenge bata rahe hai hum tumko, sara chinarpanti abhiye nikal denge…

Chillua

Pehle apna lalla ko samjhao, fir humko dekhna.

Murari Ji

Pata nai ka karega jivan me.

12 Ext. ROAD - Day 12

Gagan and Mukesh walking on the streets.

GAGAN

Love marriage karunga.

MUKESH

Kahe? Love marriage me aisa kya hai.

Aue waise bhi ee sab ameer aadmi ka chochle hain, hum jaiso ki shaadi ho jaaye wahi badi baat hai.

GAGAN

Bade boring type ke ho be. Humko to chahiye ek sundar si ladki…

Jiske jhil jaisi aankhon me doob jaane ka man kare, jiske julphon ke neeche soh jaen toh zamane bhar ki neend puri ho jaaye…

Hume love marriage isliye karna hai kyun ki… kyun ki…

MUKESH

Shahrukh khan banne ka khujali hai?

GAGAN

Haan… chuo bey

Mukesh

Ladki paise se patati hai, kamayi ke maamle mein toh nil batta sanata ho, phir kaise hoga?

Gagan

Papa jaisa mat bolo, sal gareeb aadmi. Humme toh mil hi jaayegi mere sapno ki rani.

Mukesh

Ji maharaj… pudiya khilao… esi baat par

Gagan and Mukesh cross the road and stand nearby eating Gutkha when they see a big group of people carrying a banner for cleanliness campaign.

The group walks slowly in silence in front. Gagan is about to spit out the Gutkha in his mouth but stops suddenly when he sees Anaya for the first time in the crowd.

The group reaches near Gagan and there is some waste nearby blocking the road and hence Anaya stops and looks at Gagan. She signals without words for Gagan to leave, but he is speechless. He doesn't say anything, so she wonders whether he is mute or why he isn't speaking.

Gagan realizes and steps aside so that the group can move on. Anaya looks at Gagan with a weird look and moves on while Gagan is still staring at her.

After the group moves on, Mukesh taps Gagan's shoulder.

Mukesh

Lagta hai mil gayi tumhari kajol.

Gagan spits out the Gutkha and looks with a sign of relief towards Mukesh.

Gagan

Ye hai kon, ek dam waisa hi jaisa hum sapna dekhte the… yaar pata karna padeaga eske baare mein…

13 Ext. GAGAN'S HOUSE (TERRACE) - Night 13

Gagan, Bablu, Mukesh are chilling on the terrace, when Gagan's grandfather suddenly interrupts them.

Dadaji

Abe hamare bina hi chalu ho gaya tum log.

Bablu

Dadu aap humari girlfriend to hai nahi jo intezaar kare…

Dadaji taps Bablu on the head. Bablu shifts a bit to make place for dadaji to sit down.

Dadaji

Intzaar to tumri amma v karegi…. aukaat bhulo, mat apna… aur e na kachaa ka vyapaar tum jo kar raha hai, partner banalo humko.

Mukesh laughs out loud.

Bablu

Kachha wala baat kon bataya aapko…

Dadaji

bhutni ke… dada hai tumhare hum… humise bakarpanti?

Dadaji notices Gagan looking a bit lost and not participating in the group.

Dadaji

Ab iss sajjan ko kya takleef hai bhai.

Kaunsa naye grah ka khoj karne ka vichaar hai.

Bablu

(looking at Gagan)

Abe daru ko intezaar nahi karate. Paap lagega!

Gagan

Jo nasha humko aaj chadha hai uske samne yeh nasha kuch bhi nahi hai.

They all look towards Gagan with curiosity.

Bablu

Sukha nasha kiya hai lagta hai.

Namak soongh lia ka be? E kya gyaan pel raho ho bey.

Dadaji

Wah mera pota kitna variety ke nashe karne laga hai.

Gagan

Arre nashediyon pyaar ki baat kar rahe hai hum. Ishq ka nasha chadha hai humko.

Mukesh

Acha woh aaj wali ladki?

Dadaji leans towards Gagan in excitement.

Dadaji

Ladki mil gai? Ab iski maa ka garajana kum hoga.

Bablu

Lekin ladki hai kaun? kahan rehti hai?

Mukesh

Apne bhai ke dil me rehti hai.

Dadaji taps Mukesh on his head.

Dadaji

Esiliye kehte hai susht dimag, tumhara khud ka le leta hai….

Ghar kaha hai ladki ka.

Gagan

Ghar ka pata, pata nahi.

Mukesh

Arre toh mai lekar aaunga na pata.

Bablu

Khud ka ata pata nahi aur yeh pata lekar ayega.

Gagan looks into the clouds while the rest are still talking as the voices fade and the night turns into day.

14 Int. GAGAN'S HOUSE (BEDROOM) - Morning 14

A hand suddenly gets a hold of Gagan who was fast asleep, and he wakes up in shock to see Bablu and Mukesh at his bed side.

Bablu

Gagan… Gagan abe utho bhabhi ke bare me pata kar liye hain.

Gagan

Kaun bhabhi?

Mukesh

Abe jaldi uth Bhabi ka pata mil gaya hai.

Gagan

kya baat kar raha hai…

Bablu

sala banaras me ladki oo bhi humare pachuch se door, ye utna hi namaukin hai jitna phate hue ko fir se naya banana…

Gagan

(kisses bablu)

Dil jeet liya tum, meri jaan….

Bablu

E sab usko dena … humko sone do neend aa raha hai bahut.

Sumitra pulls the bed sheet from under Bablu.

Sumitra Devi

Are utho tumhari amma nahi aaegi chaddar dhone…

Gagan, half awake, gets up and tries to get fresh, but Mukesh pushes him to hurry. They both rush outside and leave.

15 Ext. road - Day 15

Gagan & Bablu ask a few people around about Anaya but they don't seem to know anything. There is sudden rain and Gagan gets drenched.

16 int. old age home - Day 16

Gagan & Bablu rushes into a nearby building to avoid the rains.

Bablu

Abey bhaago… jaldi… humara jeans bheeg jaega…

Gagan

Sala tum pata to sahi nikale the na… faltu ka edhar udhar dauda rahe ho…

Bablu

Ee kaise ho sakta hai bataya toh yahi tha…

There are several old people in the building seated and among them he sees Anaya who is helping one of the seniors at the old age home. Kusum is also helping out a few people and talking with Anaya.

(Musical theme)

Gagan realizes that Anaya is a social worker and admires her. Anaya also sees Gagan starring at her but ignores him. The rains now heavier than before.

cut to:

17 Ext. Road - Day 17

MONTAGE

- Gagan waits several times near the old age home for Anaya but is unable to approach her to talk. Anaya notices Gagan but ignores him.

- Gagan on the bike stops to help an old man who is arguing with a shopkeeper over his change. The old man thanks Gagan and collects his change from the shop and leaves. Gagan seems happy with himself as he sits back on the bike, unaware that Anaya who was walking nearby has seen all this. She smiles and contemplates over Gagan's actions.

- Anaya notices Gagan following him. She thinks that he might be a good guy.

18 Int/Ext. GAGAN'S HOUSE (BEDROOM/Terrace) - Night 18

Sumitraji applies oil on Gagan's hair. Murariji enters the hall giving a weird look to Gagan and then goes inside.

Gagan gets a call from Anaya and rushes to the terrace.

18A int. anaya's house (bedroom) - Night 18A

INTERCUT phone conversation of Gagan/Anaya.

GAGAN

Hello? Hello kaun

Anaya

Toh tumhare paas itna unknown number se phone aata hai.

Gagan

Acha aap? laga nahi tha ki itna jaldi phone karengi…

Anaya

Bhut experience hai aapko… bada dhaayn rakhte hai time ka…

Gagan

Are nahi wo baat nahi hai, matlab yaha par aisa kaha dekhne milta hai! lekin acha laga humko…

Anaya

Khusi ke maare gir mat jaiyega…

GagaN

Bhut sharp hai aap… aur sundar bhi…

Anaya

Ye line kitno ko kaha hai esse pehle… kahi humne koi galti to nahi ki…

Gagan

Wo to aap bataiyega, waise hum aapko batade ki hum ek bhut hi sharif, shaant aur payaare insaan hai yakeen na ae to test kar ke dekh lijie…

Anaya

Acha khud ki itni taarif… lekin agar ye sach hai tab to ek baar aapse milna pdega…

Gagan

Toh milte hai naa…

Anaya

Badi jaldi mein hai… kya baat kal subah Ghat ke kinare miliye fir…

Gagan

Ghat par…

Anaya

Yeh Banaras hai, yahaan sab kuch ghat se hi shuru hota hai aur ghat pe khatam… Good night.

Gagan keeps the phone with a wide smile on his face.

19 Int. GAGAN'S HOUSE (HALL) - Morning 19

Krishna murari pours some water from a hand-pump into a bucket and goes towards the washroom while Sumitra devi is sweeping the lawn. Gagan all dressed up rushes past them in a hurry.

Murari Ji

Kaha chali sawari subeh-subeh?

Sumitra Devi

Lalla tabiyat pani sab theek to hai na?

Dadaji

Subeh uthe to dikkat, na uthe to dikkat. Ghar se nikalte samay kisiko toka mat karo tum log…

Dadaji gives Gagan some money while winking and smiling at him. Gagan takes the money and leaves happily.

20 Ext. ROAD - Day 20

MONTAGE - INTERCUT Gagan/Anaya

- Gagan is walking towards the ganga ghat.
- He climbs the boundary wall of a neighboring house and looks around.
- He breaks a few flowers and makes a bunch of them and leaves.

20A Ext. ROAD - Day 20A

- Anaya steps into an e-rickshaw.

- The wind blowing into her hair while she smiles.
MONTAGE ENDS

21 Ext. GANGA GHAT - Day 21

Anaya arrives at Ganga ghat with a small packet in her hand and steps out. She takes a seat and waits for Gagan.

In the meanwhile, Gagan reaches the ghat and looks around for Anaya until he sees her seated at one of the corners.

He sits a bit away from her rather shyly but she notices him.

Gagan

Hello

Anaya

Hi!

Gagan

Kaphi saalo baad itna subah utha, jyada intezaar to nahi karaya na humne?

He moves closer to her.

Anaya

Pehle hume laga ki tum bas time pass kar rahe ho, Lekin tumhari consistency dekh ke laga ki mil lena chahiye…

Gagan

(smiling)

pehli baar kisse mil rahe hai, pata nahi tha kya lae raste me ye dikha, badi mehnat se lekar aaye hai, soche tumko pasand aaega…

Gagan gives the flowers he picked to Anaya.

Anaya

Bhut sundar hai… humko aaj tak aise koi phool nahi diya…. College mein thhe hum, ek ladka bhut acha lagta hai, naadan thhe, pyaar ho gaya tha humko. Tumko pta hai us rishe mein sirf hum the wo to tha hi nahi, pta hi nahi chala ki kab hum uske itna kareeb aa gaye… aur wo kisi aur ke… hum uske liye sirf ek jarurat the… jo poori ho gayi fir bas aage nikal jao…

Gagan

Hum na humesa ek sapna dekhe hai, us sapna mein ek bhut sundar ladki hoti hai tumhari bilkul tumhari tarah … hum usse ghanto baat kiya karte hai, uska haath pakad ke pura sahar ghumte hai, ek dum hero wala feel aata tha… fir tum dikhi, us rally mein, aisa laga jaise sapna se nikal kar tum saamne aa gayi aur hum tumko dekhte reh gaye… chahe kuch bhi ho, hum tumko kabhi hurt nahi hone denge Anaya…

Anaya

(looking at him continuously)

Ek baar hurt ho chuke hai hum tum ache lagte ho humko agar hum sach me tumko ache lagte hai tabhi aage aana… nahi to rishta aur bhi hota hai, kam se kam ummed to nahi rahega…

Gagan

(moves his hand forward)

Aage to hum aa chuke hai Anaya… ek baar bharosa karo humpe…

Anaya

Thik hai, lekin uske baad tum humko bura banaras ghumaoge…

Gagan

100%

Anaya hugs Gagan, who also slowly wraps his arms around her warmly.

22 Ext. GANGA GHAT - Day 22

SONG 2 - Romantic Song as per choreography.

23 Ext. Gutkha FACTORY - Day 23

Mukesh reaches the Gutkha factory and joins the other workers. Several workers are picking and loading some materials into the factory. Kishore is eating some Gutkha while he abuses his workers.

Kishore

(pulls in a breath)

E hua na asli maal… mahak itna acha hai, khane wala sab humara naam na le to kehna.

Krishna (worker)

Sahi keh rahe hai bhaiya jee… ek paaket mein aadmi jhum jaega… baaki bhaiya humko ek baat samajh me nahi aa raha hai…

Aaj kal ka jo young generation hai jyada hi kabeel ho raha hai… ee sab jagah-jagah abhiyaan nikalte jaa raha hai…

Kishore

(wipes his face)

Nikalne do… nasha jitna sasta hota hai na utna mushkil hota hai usko chodhna… kucho nahi hoga e sab bakaeti se.

Krishna (worker)

Ji bhaiya ji… aap na bhute jyada tez hai.

Kishore

Makhan kam pelo kaam ka bolo.

Krishna (worker)

Bhaiya ji oo na humko thoda paisa karwa dete naa… sunday ko filim laga hai soche hai biwi ko dikha aaye…

Kishore

Kaam par mann lagao bey… chutiye… Cinema dekhana hai.

Mukesh greets Mr. Kishore the factory manager as he passes by.

Mukesh

Pranam Bhaiya ji…

Kishore

Hmm… sara delavery ho gaya… bdhiya kaam kar rahe ho tum…

Mukesh

(happily)

Thank you bhaiya ji…

Kishore leaves from there.

24 Ext. GAGAN'S HOUSE (TERRACE) - Night 24

Gagan has a few drinks while discussing Anaya with his friends Bablu and Mukesh.

Mukesh

U tumko kaam ke bare me puche, par tum to bekaar ho… usko daru, Gutkha, khaini se nafrat hai, joh tum pura shiddhat se karte ho.

Abey tum toh uske criteria mein hi fit nahi aa rahe ho bey.

Bablu

Es chirandu ki baat mat sun bhai… e sab se kuch nahi hota hai… tum bas feel karo

kya bey sahi kahe na…

Mukesh

Bhak…

They are interrupted by a call on Gagan's phone. He is surprised to see a call from Anaya.

Gagan

Anaya ka phone hai…

Bablu

Uthao-uthao… Speaker pe…

Gagan moves to the side to take the call.

Anaya (V.O)

Kal kya kar rahe ho?

Gagan

Kuch nahi bas aise hi.

Anaya (V.O)

Toh fir milte hai kal

Gagan

Kal… haan-haan bilkul matlab hum bhi wahi kehne wale thhe.

Kal na hum tumko ek dam badhiya wala ras madhuri khilate hai, ek dam best hai yaha ka.

Anaya (V.O)

Tum na ek dam buddhu ho, humesa aisa hi milna hai?

Gagan

Aise hi matlab, aise hi toh milte hai na.

Anaya (V.O)

Kahi aise jagah mile jaha pe halla gulla kam ho, kahi akele mein jaha bas hum aur tum ho.

Gagan looks in a confused manner at his friends as the call ends.

MUKESH

Kya boli?

Gagan

Akele me milne bol rahi hai.

Bablu

Kya baat hai, beta chaa gaye tum to

Gagan

(feeling a bit shy)

Abey hum nervous ho jaate hai…

Bablu

Abe akal se paidal manusaya tum na jyada socho mat, kahe ki wo tumse hoga nahi… kaha miloge…

Gagan

Puch to sala aise rahe ho jaise hum roz kaand kiye firte hai…

Mukesh

Pressure mat lo, tum bas normal raho…

Gagan

Phatt rahi hai be humari.

Bablu

(holding his nose)

Tum na anlom bilom karo…

Gagan

Tumhi karo… kaha bulaye…

Mukesh

Let me think.

Bablu

Ho gaya soch liye… sharam aana chahie humare hote hue tum log…

Shamed on you two.

Gagan

Aacha batao…

Bablu whispers in Gagan's ear and he blushes at the suggestion.

25 Ext. MEDICAL SHOP - Day 25

Mukesh & Bablu are forcing Gagan to go inside the chemist shop to buy a safety. Gagan nervously enters the chemist shop and waits at the counter.

GAGAN

Bhaiya zara woh dena.

chemist

Yahan 1760 kisam ke woh hain, Aapko kaunsa woh chahiye.

Gagan

Arre helmet chahiye Bhaiya.

Chemist

Helmet wahan samne wale dukaan me milega.

Gagan

Woh wala helmet nahi yaar.

The chemist steps closer towards Gagan.

Chemist

Acha woh wala helmet… first time hai na?

Gagan

Aapko kaise pata?

Chemist

Beta 20 saal se yahi dhanda kar rahe hain… aur yeh goli bhi lelo… aadhe ghante pehle le lena… Ek dum tan tana tan-tan

Gagan buys it and leaves feeling a bit shy.

26 Int. FRIEND'S HOUSE - Day 26

Gagan, Mukesh & Bablu goes to the house of his friends where Gagan finds the house decorated like a honeymoon setup.

Gagan

Tumhara dimag tumhar ghutna me hai kya bey… tum sala aisa intezaam karke rakho ho… pata nahi sochegi humare baare mein.

Bablu

Munna ee sab experience ka khela hai, jyada nervousao mat… ladki ko pasand aata hai bey ee sab.

Gagan

kon ladki… sala tum jis bhi ladki se setting kie ho, tumre tarah ki hai, abey oo padhi likhi ache ghar ki ladki hai…

Mukesh

Wow ee wala hum video mein dekhe thhe, pehente kaise hai… esko.

Mukesh picks up a handcuff, and Gagan tucks it under his pillow.

Gagan

Hum jaa rahe hai… humse nahi hoga.
Gagan gets angry at Bablu and decides to leave from there but sees Anaya climbing up the stairs. Mukesh & Bablu leave. Gagan retreats to the room quickly.
The room is decorated with hues of red and pink. The room contains a bed, a side table, a few chairs and flowers stuck to the walls and furniture which give the room a pleasant fragrance and atmosphere.
Gagan places a gift he had purchased for Anaya on a table, fidgeting with its placement and murmuring how he will give the gift to her when she arrives.
There is a knock on the door, and Gagan opens the door. He gets nervous as he sees Anaya smiling back at him. He asks her to come in and as she walks in, she is surprised at the level of decoration done inside.
Anaya
Dikhne mein to tum ek dam shareef se ho, yaha toh kuch aur hi deekh raha hai.
Gagan
Are nahi wo Bablu… mera matlab hai hum zoche thoda room ko sundar se saza de… Acha nahi laga na…
Anaya
(smiling)
bhut acha laga… kaphi romantic wala feel aa raha hai
Gagan
Acha tumhare liye kuch laye hai
(gives her the gift)
Yeh tumhare liye.
She smiles on seeing the gift. She starts to kiss him but after a minute, he gets very nervous and gets up asking to go to the bathroom.
Gagan

(signals to use the bathroom)

Hum abhi aaye…

Gagan goes to the bathroom while Anaya opens up the gift and has a big smile on her face. Back in the bathroom, Gagan is very nervous and searches his pockets for a packet of Gutkha. He pours the entire packet in his mouth and feels a sense of relief, but then spits it into the bathroom sink, a few beads get stuck in the sink, and he tries to clean it out of fear that she may see it, when she uses the bathroom. He cleans his mouth and comes out.

Gagan is hesitant but readily agrees and sits with Anaya on the side of the bed.

Anaya

Tum nervous ho?

Gagan

Nahi woh thoda… matlab pehle aisa kabhi hua nahi… kyun ki tum itni cute ho toh…

Anaya kisses Gagan but he moves back rather suddenly which makes her feel strange. However, she suspects something and hence moves closer to Gagan. The smell of Gutkha is very obvious. This angers her changing her mood instantly.

Anaya

Tumne kya khaya hai… Tum ye sab khake hume kiss kar rahe ho?

Sach mein…

Gagan

Anaya hum samjhate hai.

Anaya

Tumne humse jhut bola… esliye hum bharosa karne se darte thhe, tum saare ladke na ek hi tarah ke hote hai… eske alawa aur kuch nahi chahie hota…

Gagan

Hum tumko batane wale thhe?

Anaya

Bata toh diya…

Gagan has no words to reply and bows his head down in shame. Anaya leaves in anger while Gagan tries to stop her.

Gagan

Humari baat suno Anaya.

Gagan

Anaya please… Anaya… Anaya…

Gagan follows Anaya through the stairs and pleads her to wait and listen, but there is nothing left to be heard or understood, as Anaya walks away without a word.

CUT TO:

27 Ext. Bittu'S PAAN SHOP - Afternoon 27

Gagan returns dejected to his friends, who are waiting to hear about his time with Anaya.

Bablu

Abey itni jaldi aa gaya?

Doodh ke sath chhuhare, badam wagera liye kar. Aur kuch nahi pehli baar thoda sa pradarshan chaap rehta hai… Abey matlab performance pressure.

Gagan

Sab gadbad ho gaya yaar…

Gagan

Anaya gusse hokar chali gayi.

Usko pudia khane wala log ek dam nahi pasand abhi thodi der pehle mere muh se pudiya ka smell aa gaya aur woh chali gayi.

Mukesh

Pudia hi toh sungha hai Tatti thodi aur etna sa baat pe tumko chor ke chali gayi… bhai kaha pudiya kaha ladki… Chodho yaar usko lo dabao… bhut aaegi guru chodo…

gagan

Bas tum jaise doston ke wajeh se aaj hume yeh din dekhna pad raha hai.

Tum log nahi hote toh hum aaj pudia nahi chaba rahe hote aur Anaya hume chodke nahi jaati.

Mukesh

Abe oh, pudia khana hum tumko seekhaye hai… saale ishq ladao tum aur ladki ka pata dhunde hum, tumhare liye sej sajaye hum aur ladki tumse nahi sambhali toh tum wapas aakar hum hi ko pelogey. Wah ji wah…

Gagan

Hum ab se hum pudia chod rahe hai.

Bablu

Bhai ek baar aur vichar karlo ladki ke liye pudia chod dena uchit nahi hoga.

Gagan leaves without any further thoughts.

Bittu

Beta pudia chodhne se pehle udhari chuka dena humara, samaj sewa mein nahi baethe hai hum.

Bablu

Isko ka ho gaya hai?

Bittu

Kuch nahi cinema bahut dekhta hai. Yeh usika asar hai.

28 Int. GAGAN'S HOUSE - Day 28

Mukesh gets a book for Gagan containing 21 ways to quit Gutkha. Gagan looks at the book and then Mukesh.

Bablu

Ab dekho jab tum soch hi liye ho toh thik hai… aaj tak tumhare saath khade rahe hai hum, aage bhi rahenge…

Ek baat batao kya sach mein tum nahi khaoge…

Gagan

Tumko mazak lag raha hai.

Bablu

Thik hai fir… toh ye pakdo.

Gagan

Kya hai ye.

Mukesh

Pudiya chorne ka upay… pura khoj ke laaye hai…

QUICK Montage:

- Gagan marks a date on his calendar as his quit date.

28A INT. GAGAN'S HOUSE - Day 28A

Bablu gets cinnamon sticks to chew and Gagan tries but makes a weird face, Bablu and Mukesh both laugh, but also force him to continue, he chews the stick not liking it.

29 Int/Ext. Doctor's Clinic - Day 29

Bablu takes Gagan to a local doctor for help with quitting Gutkha.

Bablu

Doctor saab inka pudiya ka latt chudwana hai.

Doctor

(spits out Gutkha)

Aaan…

B1ablu

Inke latt chudwani hai.

Doctor

Kis chiz ka…

Mukesh

Pudiya, lali

Doctor

Haa to nikalo 1000 ki paata…

Bablu

Pehle upay to batao chacha…

Doctor

(chews)

mmm… bhut asaan hai, ek saath itna khao ki kahte khate mann bhar jae… hum bhi wahi kar rahe hai… ek dum kaam karega…

Gagan

kaha le kar aa gaye tum log humko, ye buddha thik karega…

Doctor

Tamiz se baat karo, humare clinic me ho tum…

Gagan

Tel lene gaya tameez, yahi patak ke marenge… bata de rahe hai…

Mukesh

Aakramak mat ho bhai, Anlom bilom karo…

Gagan

Bhaad me gaya tumhara Anlom bilom, hum khudai dekh lenge…

Gagan seems frustrated with this failed attempt.

30 EXT. Govt. CollEge - Day 30

Gagan waits for Anaya and on seeing her leave the college gate, follows her. She is with her friends. Gagan approaches and tries to stop her but she keeps walking.

Gagan

Anaya hum pura kosis kar rahe hai, ek baar humari baat suno… hum jaldi se jaldi e sab chor denge… bahut pyaar karte hai tumse…

Anaya

Yaha tamasa mat banao… humko tumse koi baat nahi karna hai, humara peecha mat karo. Hum request kar rahe hai tumse.

Anaya doesn't talk with him and leaves from there. Gagan gets upset.

31 int. Bittu'S PAAN SHOP - Day 31

Gagan tries to avoid having Gutkha but his urge is very strong and he has a packet of Gutkha but spits it out midway, throwing the remaining of the packet on the ground as he leaves feeling upset.

32 int. old age home - Day 32

Anaya is thinking of Gagan and whether she should meet him. An old man comes up to her.

old man

Arre Anaya beta?

Anaya

Ji dada ji, kuch chahiye aapko?

Old Man

Nahi-Nahi hum toh bas keh rahein hai woh babua aata raha tumre sang, Haan Gagan, oo dikh nahi raha aaj kal? sab theek toh hai?

Anaya is slightly upset while thinking about Gagan.

33 int. GAGAN'S HOUSE (VERANDA) - Day 33

Gagan is in the veranda doing yoga with full concentration. His parents start arguing and his grandfather tries to calm them down.

Murari Ji

Arre sumitra tere bete ko bhoot pret lag gaya kya? Samanye manushya jaisi harkatein nahi hai iska.

Dadaji

Achha toh tere hisaab se bhoot pret, yog aasan karte hain.

Sumitra Devi

Haan nahi toh, Jab dekho mere bete ke peeche haath dhoke pade rehte hain yeh.

Murari Ji

Arre hum toh isliye keh raha tha ki hame hazam nahi ho raha hai iska badlav.

Gagan overhears this and gets irritated and leaves the home.

34 ext. Bittu'S PAAN SHOP - Day 34

Gagan walks by Bittu's paan shop and sees the packets of Gutkha with love and also sadness that he has to quit it. He walks by again and again, every time getting more sad.

Bittu

(laughing)

Kya munna, khaoge….

Gagan gets irritated by Bittu and moves on cursing Bittu.

35 int. GHat (ghanta chacha) - Day 35

Gagan is talking to Chillua on Ghat about his urge. Chillua takes Gagan to meet Ghanta chacha.

Ghanta chacha

Beta daru, Mahua, Cigarette, Tambakoo sabka illaj hai par gutkha ka sasuri kauno illaj nahi ba…

Par ek upay hai meri jaankari me. Ek sidha purush hai. Sadak chhaap baba samajhne ki bhool na karna. Humre swayam ke gutkhe ki latt unhone chhudai thi. Bada gyaani hai baba.

Chillua

(leaning forward)

Aur ee baba milengey kahan?

ghanta chacha

Ishwar kaha milte hain?

Chillua

Mandir mein!

Ghanta Chacha

Prani matra ke mann me ishwar vas karte hain. Ussi antar mann ki gehrayon me jhaak kar dekhega, Baba zaroor milenge!

Gagan and Chillua leave and talk after moving a bit further.

Gagan

Yeh antarmann google map pe batata hai kya?

Chillua nods with no idea as to what to reply.

Gagan

Phir kaha dhoodhengey baba ko?

36 Ext. TEMPLE - Day 36

Gagan and Chillua meet the baba finally after some searching. He tells Chillua to wait, while he takes Gagan with him inside a cave like temple.

37 Int. GAGAN'S HOUSE (VERANDA) - Day 37

Gagan comes home after sometime in a new avatar, wearing prayer beads on his neck, hair combed behind, and looking like a sadhu.

His family are shocked looking at him. Chillua enters afterwards.

Sumitra Devi

Ee ka haal bana rakha hai babua aur kitne dino se nahaye nahi ho?

Gagan

Hume ab inn sansarik kriyaon ko karne ki koi avashyakta nahi hai kum se kum 7 dino tak.

Chillua

Chachi aap chinta mat karo ab isne na gyaan prapt kar liya hai. Abb yeh doosra shankaracharya banega.

Sumitra Devi

Arre kidde phade tum logo ko, hum ise dulha banana chah rahi hu aur tum log shankaracharya bana rahe ho.

Chillua

Nahi-nahi chachi aap samjhe nahi… Yeh saara khel dulha banne ke liye toh ho raha hai.

Sumitra Devi

Aaan?

Gagan goes to the side and pulls a mat for doing Yoga. His mother is shocked. Gagan's grandfather tells her to calm down.

38 int. GAGAN'S HOUSE (BedRoom) - Night 38

Murariji is busy searching for something in a drawer when his wife enters the bedroom.

Sumitra Devi

Yeh Gagan ko ka hua hai, bahut behki-behki harkatein kar raha hai.

Murari Ji

Uss din jab mai bol raha thha kaise chaddh gayi thi mere upar yaad hai?

Sumitra Devi

Arre hum toh aise hi bol rahe thhe. Hum kya bol rahe thhe, aap tanik usse baat kariye na?

Murari Ji

(looking in a drawer for something)

Arre kuch nahi nautanki kar raha hai. Do chaar din me line pe aa jayega wapas.

Sumitra Devi

Sun rahe hai, humko na bhut tension ho raha hai…

Murariji stops searching and turns towards Sumitra.

Murari Ji

Ab kya hua…

Sumitra Devi

Lalla aaj kal aisa-aisa harqat kar raha hai, humko to kuch samajhe mein nahi aa raha hai…

Murari Ji

Jyada socho mat BP badh jaegi, hum dekhte hai kya hai… ee pankha ko kya hua.

The fan is slowly rotating, Murariji goes to sleep, while Sumitra devi looks at the ceiling.

39 Ext. liquor shop - night 39

Bablu and Mukesh are at liquor shop buying booze.

Bablu

Aaj bhute badhiya mood me hai hum… 2 bottle aur de do… Lao paisa lao bey…

Mukesh is upset about something and Bablu tries to talk but he is not in the mood.

40 ext. GAGAN’S HOUSE - Night 40

They reach near Gagan’s home after which, Mukesh refuses to join and leaves suddenly.

Bablu

E pakdo tum lekar upar jao… hum gaadi laga dete hai…

Mukesh

Hum ghar jaa rahe hai, kuch kaam hai humko.

Bablu

Jyada bhaav mat khao bey… tumko kon sa kaam hai abhi…

Mukesh leaves in an irritated mood.

41 Int. MUKESH'S HOUSE - Night 41

Mukesh arrives home and meets his mother.

Mukesh's Mother

Khaana rakhe hain, kha lo.

Mukesh takes a few utensils containing food and starts eating.

Mukesh

E lo es mahina ka…

She throws the vessel in her hand in anger.

Mukesh's Mother

Bas itna hi…

Mukesh

Amma yaar tum fir se chalu mat jao… hum bhi to thoda kharcha hai na, hum kon sa sarkari naukari kar rahe hai

Mukesh's Mother

Sahi hai, hum hi sambhale sab…

(crying)

tumhara baap to bhaag gaya, aur rah gaye hum… din bhar dusra ka kaam karte hai, aedi shooj jata hai lekin tumko samajh mein aaye tab na.

Maa mar jaye bolte-bolte tumko to ayaasi karna hai na, apna dost log ke saath. Karzdaar sab na mera jaan nikalta hai, hum sunte hai un sab ka gaali, lekin tumko kya hai apna-apna socho sab, e bhi thik hai.

Mukesh stops eating for a moment and looks at his mother.

Mukesh

Hum bhi to mehnat kar rahe hai na, chori thodi kar lenge jaake amma…

(talks loudly)

Hum kya kare tum hi batao… humko acha lagta hai tum sabka jhutan maanjti ho… lekin kare kya hum….

Mukesh's Mother

Hum aisa kab kahe tumko, humko bhi to dekho

Mukesh

Tumko bhi yahi lagta hai na ke hum papa jaise hai, hum nahi hai unki tarah… nahi hai hum…

Mukesh pushes the plate aside. He goes to his room while his mother sits back crying.

42 Ext. Bittu'S PAAN SHOP - Day 42

Bablu is seated at the paan shop talking to Bittu and having Gutkha, when Gagan comes up to him.

Bittu

(talking to a customer)

Kapad phod denge hum tumhara, bakaeti mat batiyao humse. 3 mahina se bol raha hai de denge, de denge kab dega humare nikal lene ke baad…

Gagan

Mukesh kaha hai, 2 din se koi ata pata nahi hai… phone bhi nahi utha raha hai…

Bablu

Hum kasam bata rahe hai ek din hum bittu bhaiya ko ulta latka ke marenge…

Gagan

Chalo dekh ke aate hai.

They both leave towards Mukesh's home.

43 Ext. GAGAN'S HOUSE (VERANDA) - Day 43

There is a knock on the door and dadaji responds.

DADAJI

Bahu dekho toh kaun hai darwaze pe.

SUMITRA DEVI

Ji bauji ayi…

(opens the door)

Ji kahiye?

ANAYA

Aunty gagan ghar pe hai?

SUMITRA DEVI

Beta aap kon?

ANAYA
Aunty hum Gagan ke dost hai.
Sumitra Devi
Acha-acha… Beta andar aao na.
Anaya enters the house and greets the family.
Dadaji
Acha beta, tumhara naam kya hai?
Anaya
Ji, Anaya
Sumitra Devi
Beta tum baitho hum chai, Biscuit lekar aate hai.
Anaya
Nahi-nahi aunty hum bas Gagan se milkar chale jaayenge.
44 ext. MUKESH'S HOUSE - Day 44
Mukesh is on a cycle and about to leave when Bablu and Gagan meet him.
Gagan
Kaha gayab ho bey… 2 din ho gaya… na ata na pata…
Mukesh ignores them.
Bablu
Oo garib aadmi … bhaav kya kha rahe ho bey…
Gagan
kuch hua hai kya tumko, koi kuch bola hai
Mukesh
kon bolega humko, aur kahe hi bolega… tum log ke liye hum kya hai… kya faraq padta hai, bhale zindagi humari maar le… garib hona na aaj ke date me sabse bada paap hai, ek time par apna sala dost bhi puchna band kar deta hai.
Gagan
Sathiyagaye ho kya tum, kya bakarpanti kiye hue ho tabse, seedha bolo baat kya hai…

Mukesh
Hum bakarpanti kie hue thik hai, hum hi to chutiya hai, sala mohobbat karo tum, upay lagaye hum, kaand karo tum, sudhare hum, tumhara chamcha nahi hai hum… jo tumhare peeche-peeche ghumega… kabhi soche ho, humara kya, humare zindagi mein kya cahl raha hai…
Bablu
Bhai hota hai, sabka life mein problem hai, log kosis kar raha hai…
Mukesh
Tum kya bole raha hai, tumhara apna koi stand hai, 1 paisa to jeb se nikalta nahi hai, jab bole muh bana lete ho, khali fashion se zindagi nahi katta hai… aur ye, kal ki aayi ladki ke liye pudiya chorne chale, 2 din to tika nahi paaye baat karta hai…
Gagan slaps Mukesh and he has tears in his eyes.
Gagan
(feeling angry and guilty)
Jaaoo…
Gagan tries to stop Mukesh but he leaves in a rage, so does Gagan. Bablu is shocked looking at his friends leave like that, not knowing what to do next.
45 Int. GAGAN'S HOUSE (TERRACE) - Afternoon 45
Gagan comes home in angry & started meditating when someone drops a bucket of water onto him. He gets irritated and sees that it is his father. He dusts the water from his head and body.
Murari Ji
Pagla gaye ho ka? Ee sab ka harkat kar rahe ho? Bhai aggar tumhe sansaar tyaagke sadhu banna hai toh ee ghar chodh doh aur jaakar kisi math mein baith jao.

Humare ghar mein ee sab nahi chalegi. Yaha rehna hai toh kayda mein rahna hoga.

Gagan moves closer to his father.

Gagan

Kaunsa ghar? Bol toh aise rahe ho jaise khud banwaye ho ee ghar ko. Na hi ghar aapka hai aur na hi dhandha. Sab aapko virasat mein mila hua hai. Aapne khud ka kiya kya hai zindagi mein.

Murariji is silent and shocked at Gagan's words.

Gagan

Woh chodhiye humare mere liye kiya ka hai aaj tak, badi badi baat karalo ense bas, Zara apne aap ko dekhiye.

Aap ek hare hue insaan hain, hare hue aur majboor insaan , toh apne gyaan ka peti apne paas rakhiye aur hume apni zindagi jeene dijiye…. haath jorte hai hum aapse.

Gagan leaves in anger while Murariji keeps looking at him, with tears in his eyes.

46 Ext. Bittu'S PAAN SHOP - Afternoon 46

Gagan comes to Bittu's pan shop and breaks all the prayer beads he was wearing in anger.

Gagan

Pudia khila Bittu bhaiya.

Bittu

Bas huyi gaya, Karli kosish. Nahi choota pudiya. 15 saal ho gaya yahan dhanda karte-karte.pudia ki latt lagte dekha hai bahut logo ko lekin choota kisi ka bhi nahi.

Gagan

Aisa hai Bittu mastak mera hai kharab, dimaag ka taapman room temperature se bhi zyaada hai.

Isliye apni Amar chitra katha bandh karo aur pudia khillao.

Gagan consumes a little gutkha when he stops suddenly. Anaya is just opposite to Gagan and he is shocked to see her there. He spits the gutkha out while she comes to him and starts saying ill things to him.

Anaya

You are so much predictable.

Gagan

Anaya humari baat suno.

Anaya

Ab sunane ko baaki kya bacha hai?

Humari soch tumko leakr ek dam sahi thi, inn mohalle walo par kabhi bharosa mat karna, Tum jaise log pyaar aur bharose ke Qaabil nahi hote.

Par hum apne aap ko samjhaye ladd pade, kahe ki humara dil kehta tha ki nahi yaar ladka acha hai chor dega lekin …..

(Takes in a breath)

Tumne humara bharosa toda hai, Gagan. Tum jaise log na bas pyaar ka mazak banana jaante hai, humko khud pe gussa aa raha hai ke hum tumhare baato mein kaise aa gaye?

Gagan

Hume samjhane ka mauka toh do ek baar.

Anaya

Hum aaj ke baad kabhi nahi milenge.

Gagan is continuously getting calls from Bablu.

She leaves from there but walks slowly hoping Gagan will come up to her and apologize. She hears Gagan talking on the phone and turns back.

He has a shocked look on his face and leaves in a hurry.

INTERMISSION

47 Int. HOSPITAL (WARD) - Afternoon 47

As soon as Gagan reaches the hospital, he sees Mukesh hurt badly on the hospital bed. His face is bruised and he is hurt very badly. Mukesh is unconscious.

Gagan
Ee sab kaise hua?
Bablu
Bahut khoon beh gaya yaar,
Aath Dus logon ne milkar maara hai
Gagan
Abe kaun hai, kisne maara puri baat batayega
Bablu tells him about all that happened.
BEGIN FLASHBACK
48 Int. Gutkha FACTORY - Day (Flashback)
48
Mukesh reaches the factory where gutkha is being produced. He meets up with Kishore (man in his early 40s), sporting a big gold chain who is the supervisor talking with another worker.
worker
Bhaiyaji yeh supaari saara sadh gayi hain aur zarde me bhi faphoondi lag gayi hai.
Kishore
Toh?
Worker
Bhaiya ji pura batch kharab ho jayega.
Kishore
Toh tumhara kon sa nuksaan ho raha hai, aur sab kar raha hai na.
Worker
Nahi bhaiya ji hum toh bas…
Mukesh hides and starts recording the conversation on his phone camera.
Kishore
Suno be harishchandra ki aulaad. Dhandha chahe milawat ka kyun na ho, Imaan me milaavat nahi honi chahiye aur

humara imaan hai paisa.
(grabs a hold of the worker's collar)
Supaari sade huye hain ilsiye sasta me mila. Waise bhi laal paani me doobne ke baad sara ka sara supari ho jaati hai.
Dana-dana ek samaan…
(leaving the collar)
Samjhe gobar prasad?
Mukesh unknowingly hits into a bucket nearby and they hear the sound.
Kishore
Kaun hai be?
Mukesh
Bhaiya hum mukesh.
Kishore
kaun Mukesh
Mukesh
Bhaiya hum hi aapka maal uthate hai.
Kishore
Toh eehan kahe udhan macha rahe ho?
Mukesh
Nahi hum toh bas maal uthane aya the aap logon ko baase karte suna toh hume raha nahi gaya.
Kishore
Saala savita bhabi ka manohar kahaniyan jok suna raha hu joh raha nahi gaya.
Mukesh
Par bhaiya logo ke saath khilwaad karna… E toh galat hai na?
Kishore
(laughing)
sala aaj kuch hai kya, sab ke muh mein boli phoot raha hai…

Abe gutkha banate hai hum, chawanprash nahi aur isse keval wahi log khata hain jinko apna ghanta farak nahi padta…

Chal beta bahut kaam pada hain.1..2..3 ke andar hiran holo

Mukesh

Bhaiya agar aapne yeh sab nahi roka toh acha nahi hoga.

Kishore

Teri maa ki…

(in an angry and loud tone)

Bhosadike tum humko dhamki de raha hai dadu pandey ko?

Tumhara chaati cheer ke yahi namak bhar denge, rafu chakkar ho lo.

Mukesh

Bhagogey toh ab aap bhaiya jab police sadak pe nanga karke daudayegi. yeh video dekh raha hai, hum seedha police ke paas jaenge esko lekar fir batate hai aapko.

Mukesh leaves in a hurry. Kishore signals to his workers to follow him.

49 Ext. ROAD - DAY (FLASHBACK) 49

Mukesh is cycling fast on the road while trying to see if anyone is following him. He realizes he is not alone and thus starts running but he stops midway due to his coughing and they catch up with him.

They beat him up badly and also snatch his phone.

Kishore

Dubaara hamre saamne phantom bane na toh patlun ke upar laal kachha pahinake superman bana denge, bahut bekhauf aadmi hai hum beta jaanlo…

Kishore breaks Mukesh's phone by stamping it. They leave him half dead as he falls unconscious on the streets.

END FLASHBACK

50 Int. HOSPITAL (lobby) - Afternoon 50

Gagan gets very angry hearing all this and leaves for the Gutkha Factory.

BABLU

Abey tum kaha jaa rahe ho?

GAGAN

Dadu ki maiyat nikalne…

Mukesh ko hosh aye toh bolna jitna khoon baha hai dadu ke sharir me utna bhi nahi chodunga.

Gagan leaves and a nurse enters the room.

Nurse

Ye kuch aur zaruri tests hain. Turant karane padengey.

Bablu

Itne saare tests humne school me diya hota to aaj hum khud doctor hote.

Nurse

Test dene se doctor nahi bante, test pass bhi karna hota hai woh bhi distinction mein.

Bablu

(to himself, as the nurse leaves)

Baat toh sahi hai.

51 Int. Gutkha FACTORY - Afternoon 51

Gagan reaches the factory and yells at the top of his voice.

GAGAN

Dadu pandey… Abey oo dum katte kuttey bahar nikal…

(shouting loudly)

DADU PANDEY!

GOON

Kaun hai bey?

Gagan

Tumhare baap… abhi apne baap, Dadu pandey ko bula.

Hearing the commotion, Kishore comes out.

KISHORE
Sar par chot lag gayi ka babua, ya dawayi galat asar kar gaya hai, Kaun ho maharaj?
GAGAN
Mukesh ko haath lagakar tum thik nahi kie…
KISHORE
Acha-acha, Saala yeh dosti bhi kutta cheez hai…
(comes close to Gagan)
Tumhaare jitna tha na tab do baar jail jaa chuke the murder case mein, bahut bada harami thhe hum
GAGAN
Tum harami thhe, hum harami hai.
Action sequence follows.
Gagan beats up all of them and finally grabs Kishore beating him up too.
GAGAN
Nikal gaya sara garmi, itna hi hunkaar tha tumhara… gurrao na… sala maza aa raha tha…
Gagan takes a glass of water and sits near Kishore who is fallen on the floor.
Gagan
Sharif insaan utna bhi sahrif nahi hota ke apna dost, parivaar ke liye ladd na sake…
Saying this Gagan leaves Kishore to his own injuries.
52 Int. HOSPITAL (loBBY) - Night 52
Gagan comes to the hospital with his torn up clothes and few wounds. He sees Mukesh's mother and Bablu sitting on a bench. They look worried.
Gagan
Kaisa hai abhi?
Bablu

Hosh toh nahi aaya ab tak. Yeh log pata nahi kya-kya jaanch kar chuke hain lekin bata koi kuch nahi raha.

Mukesh's mother starts crying and Gagan comforts her.

Gagan

Arre chachi kahe paresaan ho rahi ho, thik ho jayega Mukesh…

Aur hum sab hai na aapke saath.

The nurse calls out to them.

Nurse

Doctor saab aapko andar bula rahe hain.

53 Int. HOSPITAL (CLINIC ROOM) - NIGHT 53

All enter in the room while the doctor is checking the reports. He looks at Mukesh's Mother.

DOCTOR

Baithiye…

Gagan and the others takes a seat.

GAGAN

Bahut zyaada chot aaya hai kya?

DOCTOR

Chot toh serious hai, lekin chinta ka vishay woh nahi hai…

(moving closer towards them)

Humko aap yeh bataiye, Mukesh ka health condition kaisa tha, I mean, koi symptoms ya tabiyat kharab hone ka koi lakshan aap log ne notice kiya kabhi?

Gagan

Nahi sir, Aisa to kuch nahi hai.

DOCTOR

(looking at Mukesh's mother)

Aap Mukesh ki Maa hai?

Mukesh's Mother

Ji

Doctor

Dekhiye aapke bete ko cancer hai… 2nd stage… Mouth cancer… Aam taur par ye pudiya, tambaaku se hota hai…

They are utterly shocked and Mukesh's mother starts to cry.

Doctor

Oh immediately usse Cancer hospital shift kariye.

Mukesh's mother hugs Bablu and start crying. Gagan exits and cries near the stair case.

54 int. HOSPITAL (lobby) - Day 54

MONTAGE: Song 3 - Emotional

Mukesh's mother sits besides Mukesh, They look at each other and Mukesh understands that something is serious.

54A Ext. MEDICAL SHOP - Day 54A

Bablu is lost - He walks by a medical shop. The owner waves at Bablu and starts talking but bablu is lost in his thoughts.

54B Ext. ROAD - Day 54B

Gagan walks on road as he recalls all the childhood memories of Bablu, Mukesh and himself.

54C Ext. school - DAY (FLASHBACK) 54C

Flashback - Childhood images of the three friends playing marbles. They fight, they eat ice-lollies showing their red tongue and teasing each other, little Mukesh runs fast and the others can't catch him. They share their lunch box and laugh out loud.

54D Ext. HOSPITAL (PAAN SHOP) - Afternoon 54D

Gagan is outside the hospital & sees a few kids on the cycle buying gutkha from the paan shop and one of them is just about to eat it. He rushes and tears the packet from one of the kid's hand.

He looks at the shop and at the gutkha packets. His anger bursts and he starts snatching and tearing all the packets. He throws some money on Bittu's face.

Frustrated with all this, he sits on the road crying as the gutkha particles spread all around.

MONTAGE ENDS:

BLACK OUT:

55 Int. GAGAN'S HOUSE (HALL) - Evening 55

Krishna Murari and his wife are arguing about not knowing where Gagan has been, as they are worried about him. Murariji scolds dadaji over pampering Gagan, just when Gagan enters the house, his clothes all torn up.

Murari Ji

(angrily)

Iss ghar ko chod ke hum kahin chale jaate hai. Tab shaayad chain milega tumke bhi aur humke bhi.

Sumitra Devi

Hume toh chain anguthi kuch bhi na mila aaj tak. kum se kum aapko mil jaye usi me santosh kar lengey.

Murari Ji

Hum majaak nahi kar rahe hai. sumitra. Subah ka 10 baaj raha hain aur tumhare putra shiromani abhi tak nahi padhare ghar.

Isko ghar nahi khairaat khana ghosit kar dete hain. Jab raat- raat bhar ghar se gayab rehna hai toh.

Dada ji

Kyun rakt chaap badha rahe ho.

murari ji

Rakt chaap kya dil ka daura bhi pad jaayega ek din, iss kapooti santaan ke liye. Aur aapke laad pyaar ke wajah se hi bigada hai…

Gagan enters. Gagan hugs him tightly without saying anything and starts crying bitterly. Murariji while being surprised understands that something is deeply wrong.

GAGAN

(sobbing)

hume maaf kar dijiye papa, humse bhut badi galti ho gayi.

Murari ji hugs him back tightly.

MURARI JI

sab theek ho jayega beta. aise rote nahi

(comforting Gagan)

kya hua beta hume batao

GAGAN

Mukesh ko cancer ho gaya papa. Usko kuch nahi hona chahie papa.

Seeing this, Sumitraji also gets teary eyed and so does Dadaji.

MURARI JI

Sab theek ho jayega beta.

56 Ext. BRIDGE - Day 56

QUICK MONTAGE

Gagan and Bablu try to call their friends but no one responds, they keep trying to get some help to arrange the money.

57 Int. HOSPITAL (WARD) - Day 57

Gagan and Bablu go to visit Mukesh in the ward.

MUKESH

Abe tumko yaad hai bachpan me humlog kaise-kaise masti kiya karte thhe.

(pointing at Bablu)

Iski toh pant phatt gaya tha ek baar.

Gagan

Aur saala chaddi bhi nahi pehna tha.

They all laugh.

Bablu

Tum dono ko hamesha hum hi milte hai kya?

Mukesh

Hum teeno me sabse zayaada tumhara kata hai. Sharma sir har class me isko bench par kada kar dete thhe. Aur 24 ghanta naak iska chuta rahta tha.

Bablu

Naak chune waali baat pure Banaras me tumhi prachaar kiye ho.

Mukesh

Abe pant me joh mutt diye thhe, jab kutta peeche pad gaya tha tumhare, Woh waali baat bhi khoob prachaar kiye hai hum.

Gagan and Mukesh laugh.

Mukesh

Ek hi cycle par school jana, ek hi tiffin se khana, Chimti chachi ki baag ke amrud churana, Murari chaha ke nav par baithkar Ganga maiyya me sair karna, Achanak aankhon ke saamne sab aaraha hai.

Aaj bahut dino ke baad bachpan yaad aa raha hai.

Bittu ke baap se kitna udhari khaye hain yaar… Hahaha… Sab kuch bahut sahi jaa raha tha bas uss din woh pudiya humko nahi khana chahiye tha, Doctor kehta hai sab tambaaku pudiya se hua hai

Bada kutti cheej hai, Dekho kya halat kar diya humara.

Hum bach toh jaayengey na bey.

Gagan and Bablu hug Mukesh tightly and start to cry.

cut to:

58 Ext. BOAT - Night 58

Gagan and Bablu are tensed thinking about how they will arrange the money for Mukesh's treatment.

Gagan
Itna saare paise kaha se aayega? kuch samajh me nahi aa raha hai.
bablu
Jab hum kisi cheej me phaste thhe. Tumhi jugaad bithate thhe. Kaise bhi karke humko nikalte thhe.
Aaj humara baari hai aur hum tumko aur mukesh dono ko haarne nahi dengey. Humare pass kuch paisa hain ek baar yahi pe illaj suru karate hai.
Gagan
Wahi joh tum motorcycle lene ke liye jama kar rahe thhe?
Bablu
Saala gaadi to hazar aajaega lekin dost kaha se layenge… humare paas hai hi kon tum dono ke alawa…
Gagan keeps his hand on Bablu's shoulder and understanding the emotional situation tells Bablu.
59 Int. HOSPITAL (WARD) - Afternoon 59
Mukesh's mother sits beside Mukesh lying on the bed.
Mukesh
Kahe yahan baithi ho? Ghar jao, pareshan mat ho, hum theek ho jayengey.
mother
Tanik chup nahi reh sakte. Humko pata hai tumko kuch nahi hoga. Bhagwan do baar toh humko nahi rulayega na. Suhaag ujaad diya woh hum seh liye. Ab kokh ujaad dega toh hum kaise jeeyengey.
She cries.
60 ext. HOSPITAL (CLINIC ROOM) - Afternoon 60
Gagan and Bablu talk to the doctor.
Gagan

Sir kuch paison ka intazaam kiye hain. Aap woh homi bhaba hospital me baat kariye na.

Doctor

Kuch paison se kuch nahi hoga, Cancer ke illaj me bahut paise lagta hain. Khair thoda bahut madat mil jaayega aapko, Mediclaims aur insurance company se thoda bahut kuch cover ho jayega but anyway 9-10 lakh ka jugaad toh aapko bithana padega.

Gagan

10 lakh, itna paisa kaha se laenge sir… aap log to sabka jaan bachate hai… please kuch kijie.

Sir aisa nahi ho sakta ke hum pehle mukesh ko admit karte phir thoda bahut time leke arrange karte paisa.

Doctor

Dekhiya paisa arrange karne ke liye aapke pass sayad ek mahine ke time bhai nahi hai aur mukesh ka halat ab bigad raha hai. Jald se jald cancer ward me daalna padega.

Chemo session start karna padega immediately.

61 Int. GAGAN'S HOUSE (TERRACE) - Night 61

Gagan is lying down on his terrace alone thinking about all that is happening. He thinks about Anaya, and looks at a photo of a happy moment of them together. He tries to call her but her line is busy. His grandfather arrives there.

Dadaji

pareshaan ho? Chinta nahi-chintan karo, Sahi samasyaon ka samadhan humare andar hota hai. Dhoondne se bhagwaan mil jaate hai. samadhan nahi milega.

Gagan

Kuch samaj me nahi aa raha hai dada ji…

Bahut paisa chahiye kum se kum 8-10 lakh.

Dadaji

Kahin na kahin se ho jaayenge, Zarurat padi toh hum apni nav bech denge.

Gagan

Nav bech dogey toh hum khayemgey kya?

Dadaji

Tum bhi khane jeene ke chakaad me pad gaye. Are jab daant diya na tha tab doodh diya, Ab daat diya hai toh ann nahi dega?

Pet toh apna har koi paal leta hai bachwa manushya yoni me paida huye ho toh jeevan ke udesya ko samjho.

Apna laskya nirdharit karo aur aage badho. Waise bhi humko uss chhuchhundar ka class lagana hai. Ek baar usko theek hoke wapas aane do.

Gagan

Sirf usko kahe? Hum sab jimmedar hain. Hum sabko daatna aap?

Gagan hugs his grandfather who asks him about Anaya to change his mood.

Gagan gets a call from Bablu.

Gagan

Hello?

Bablu

Suno bey kal subeh tayyar rehna. ek jugaad mila hai. Kal milne chalna hai.

62 Int/Ext. NGO OFFICE - Day 62

Gagan and Sweety arrive at the NGO office on a bike.

Sweety

bas yahi roko… Bablu kaha hai…

Gagan calls Bablu, but he doesn't answer.

Gagan

Saala kahan reh gaya.

Bablu arrives in the meanwhile.

Sweety

Suno jitna bataya hai utna hi bolna hai. Zyadda bakaiti katayi bardast nahi karta woh…Aur tum.

(looks at Bablu)

Muh bandh rakhna gagan ko hi bolne dena. Nahi toh tum hug doge aur hume saaf karna padega.

They proceed to the NGO manager's office.

Sweety

Sir yeh Gagan hai aur yeh Bablu… humne bataya tha na?

Ngo Manager

Acha-Acha, haan kya bataya tha, Mukesh… Ab kaisi tabiyat hai uski?

Gagan

Din par din Badhta ja raha hai sir. Second stage hai sir… Papa nahi hai uske. Ek maa hai joh dusron ke gharon me bartan maajti hai.

Ngo Manager

Samaj ki raksha karna hi to humara kaam hai Aap chinta mat kariye. Hum hai na. Bas hospital ke papers, Test reports, medicine bills wagera hume sab chahiye hoga.

Gagan

(emotionally)

Are bilkul sir hum sab laake denge… Aap bas hamre bhai ko bacha lijiye.

Ngo Manager

Hum social media, News papers aur radio broadcasting ke maadhyam se logon ko appeal karenge ki woh aagey aayen aur maddat karein. Bahut sare associations hain, Cancer societies hain…

Treatment me koi kami nahi aayegi… Aap log chintamukht hoke apne dost ke pass jayiye…

Unke parivaar ke sath time spend kijiye. Baki hum dekhlenge. Bas hume video shoot karna padegaa aur kuch pictures bhi nikalne padengey.

Gagan

(with tears in his eyes)

Thank you so much sir… aap jaise log kaha milte hai.

As they are leaving, Sweety comes to take some information from Gagan and he hugs her to thank her for the help.

cut to:

Anaya and Kusum who are standing nearby below the NGO Office, see Gagan hugging Sweety.

KUSUM

Anaya wo dekho tumhara aashiq…

Anaya is shocked and angry. Anaya tries to hide her feelings as she is very upset after seeing all this.

63 Ext. GANGA GHAT - Afternoon 63

Murariji is rowing his boat and reaches the ganga ghat and parks his boat. Gagan happily runs and jumps over to help his father in setting the boat.

GAGAN

Papa lagta hai ab paison ka intajaam ho jayega.

Murari Ji

Ganga maiyya daya kare.

Gagan

Ek sajjan aadmi mile hain, Ngo chalate hain. Kahe paisa woh jugaad karengey.

customer

Kitna hua?

Murari Ji

Waise to 200 hua aapka. Lekin aaj kuch nahi lengey. Aapki aaj ki savaari humare taraf se…

The customer thanks Murariji and leaves.

Gagan

Papa hum aspatal jaa rahe hai… Mukesh ko batane.

Gagan hugs his father and leaves. Murariji searches for Chillua.

Murari Ji

Sala chillua, kidhar reh gaya… Nahi sudhrega…

64 Int. HOSPITAL (WARD) - Afternoon 64

Mukesh's mother is seated near his bed, when Gagan and Bablu arrive.

BABLU

(to Mukesh's mother)

Chachi paison ka jugaad ho gaya hai, aur insurance wala kaam ho gaya hai. Isi hafte cancer ward mein shifting ho jayega Mukesh ka.

Mukesh's mother is very relieved and happy to hear this.

Mukesh's Mother

Pehle hum ee samajhte the ki tum doston ke wajeh se hi humra beta humko samay nahi deta hai, joh bura aadat hain sab tumhare wajah se Kitna galat the mein.

Gagan hugs Mukesh's mother.

GAGAN

Arre chachi aap kahe itna sochti hain? Ee sab sochne ka samay nahi hai. Tum bas paratha khilaya karo.

Mukesh gets up and overhears the conversation.

Mukesh

Matlab tum log ka ehsaan lekar marna padega.

BABLU

(sarcastically)

Ee dekho lakkadbagha neend se jaag gaya,

Gagan

Ehsaan nahi, soodh samet nikalwaenge tumse, tum bas ghar wapas aa jao yaar.

Mukesh emotionally looking at his friends.

MUKESH

Acha bhabhi kaisi hai? Aur hum se milne kahi nahi aayi?

Gagan smiles but doesn't say anything.

65 INT. GAGAN'S HOUSE (TERRACE) - Night 65

Gagan's mother comes to meet Gagan on the terrace. She applies oil to his head. She tells him that it will all be ok.

Sumitra Devi

Tumko pata hai bachpan mein jab bhi tumko neend nahi aata tha na…

Hum tumhare maatha mein tel lagate the aur fir kya… 2 min mein tum neend mein… fir majaal hai koi kitna bhi uthale tumko…

lao hum tel laga dete hai…

Gagan

Mummy ek baat pata hai aise champi karti ho na bhut sukoon feel hota hai, man hi nahi karta kahi jaye…

Sumitra Devi

Mann khus karna koi tumse seekhe… Acha oo jo ladki ghar pe aayi thi oo kon hai, badi sundar si, pyaari si….

Gagan remembers Anaya & starts looking at her photos on his phone.

66 Int. GAGAN'S HOUSE (HALL) - Morning 66

Murari is shaving when Chillua comes to his home and tells him about the news promoted by NGO regarding Mukesh.

Chillua

Murari ji, yeh dekhe?

Murari Ji

Kya?

Chillua shows the video to Murariji and he looks surprised and calls Gagan.

MURARI JI

Gagan… beta Gagan ee dekho facebook par ishtihaar aya hai, woh NGO walon ne daala hai.

Gagan comes over.

Gagan

Acha… Dikhaiye

Murari Ji

Rukko hum padhte hai… Shashtri nagar ke 23 varshiya Mukesh bahut ko durbhagya se cancer se peedit hain. Ghar ka eklauta kamaane wala, jiska parivaar ilaaj ka kharcha uthaane ke liye asaksham hai.

Isliye aap log bhaari maatra mein aage aayey aur apne kshamta anusar madad kare

Illaj mein kum se kum 20 lakh rashi ki avashakta hain. Adhik jaankari ke liye sampark karein.

Gagan is shocked hearing this.

Murari Ji

Beta, illaj ke liye toh 8-10 lakh chahiye na, yahaan 20 lakhs kahe likh diye?

Gagan

Wahi toh hum bhi samajh nahi paa rahe hain.

Murari Ji

Arre issmein samajhna ka hai? Illaj mein kauno kami na rahe aur sab kuch badhiya se ho jaye isliye badhake likhe hongey, aise log bhagwan se kam nahi hai… tum ek kaam karo e lo

(gives a 200rs note)

jao unke liye kuch mithai le jao…

Gagan leaves to find out about all this mess.

67 Ext. ROAD - Day 67

Gagan and Bablu ride towards the NGO office.

Gagan

Yeh bahut badhia hai be.

Bablu

Kya cheej?

Gagan

Apne NGO wale bhaiya yaar, bahut ache aadmi hain…

Bablu

Bilkul, nihayat hi sajjan aadmi hain.

Gagan

Bas yaar illaj ka paisa nikal jaaye.

Bablu

Tension mat lo guru, sab theek hi hoga.

They come across a large crowd but don't stop to see what is happening.

68 Int. NGO OFFICE - Day 68

Gagan and Bablu arrive at the NGO office and open the door but are shocked to see Sweety seated on the Manager's lap.

They hide and listen to the conversation.

MANAGER

Arre Sweety meri jaan, maza aa gaya. Kya bakra phasaya ho.

The Manager and Sweety laugh out at this.

Manager

Bas aise hi bakre lekar aaya karo, phir hum itna kamayengey, itna kamayengey, tum soch bhi nahi sakti. Phir hum dono Manali chalengey.

Sweety

Gagan, Bablu, kisiko bhi iska bhanak nahi lagni chahiye.

Manager

Bhanak lag bhi gaye toh mera kya ukhad lengey?

(bringing her closer)

Acha-acha… woh tera boyfriend bablu… Usko bura na lage isliye na?

Gagan looks at Bablu and they are very angry but decide to wait a little longer and hear more of their conversation.

Sweety

Arre woh toh bas mera khilona hai…

Jaan toh aap hain huzoor… Acha kitna kama lengey?

Manager

Sab theek raha toh kum se kum 12-14 lakh. Aur 20-30 hajar uss bhikari ke muh maar dengey.

Cancer mein waisi bhi bachne ki koi guarantee nahi hai, toh jinda logon pe kharcha karo, joh marne wala hai, uspe kharcha ka, ka fayda?

Gagan barges into the room towards the Manager in anger.

GAGAN

Fayda nuksaan toh hum samjhayenge tumhe. Aur marne wala mera dost nahi balki tu hai.

Manager

Dekho tumhe knock karke aana chahiye thha.

Gagan

Oh! Hum lekin ulta karte hain, pehle kamre me ghuste hain aur phir knock kartey hain.

Gagan beats the manager, left and right. The manager also returns blows and they get into a fight.

GAGAN

Bhosadike chita pe roti sekh raha hain suar? Gareebon ka khoon chusnewala keeda.

Gagan is about to hit the Manager when Bablu stops him, and takes him on the side.

Bablu
(to Sweety)
Upar uthne ke hawas me kitna neeche gir gayi Sweety. humne sach much pyaar kiya tha, lekin tum toh mere nafrat ke bhi layak nahi ho. Jindagi bhar pyaar ke liye tarsogi…
Song music playing in the background.
69 Ext. BOAT - Night 69
Gagan & Bablu are seated on the boat & have no idea what to do next. Suddenly Gagan stands up & jump into the Ganga river. He realizes that there is no one except God who can help him.
70 Ext. KASHI VISHWANATH Temple - Afternoon 70
Gagan is praying for help to lord Shiva. Behind him people are hanging a hoarding which is about a sponsored marathon race to be held in Varanasi and has prize money of 10 lakhs. He notices it as he leaves the temple.
71 Ext. ROAD - Afternoon 71
Bablu walks behind Gagan.
BABLU
Humari baat suno bey. Hum jaante hai ki tum jeet sakta hai bachpan se tumko bhaagte dekhe hai, toh tum kahe itna soch raha hai.
GAGAN
Galli mohalle me bhagna alag hai aur competition me bhagne alag hai, se bade-bade khiladi log, joh sab har roz practice kartey hai, hum unke saath muqabla karengey?
BABLU
Kahe nahi karogey? Dost ke liye itna toh kar sakte ho na…
GAGAN

Baat woh nahi hai, training nahi hai, practice nahi hai aur competition ke liye time bhi nahi hai.

BABLU

Time toh Mukesh ke paas bhi nahi hai aur koi option nazar aa raah hai tumko…

Bablu gets a call.

72 Int. HOSPITAL (ICU) - Afternoon 72

Gagan watches Mukesh through the ICU door window.

Doctor (V.O)

Jald se jald cancer hospital shift karna padega. Chemo therapy jaldi shuru karna hai.Mukesh ka haalat bigadta jaa raha hai.

Gagan is worried about Mukesh's sudden drop in health.

BABLU

Gagan, Humko pata hai, ee asaan nahi hai, lekin guru tumko yaad hai ek chor khali tumhara pudiya gira diya tha, uske peeche tum kitna tez bhaage the jaisa tumse tumhara jayadaat le gaya…

Bharosa karo apne aap pe… tumhare andar oo baat hai bhai… tum lo hissa hum bata rahe hai…

Gagan takes a moment after hearing all this.

Gagan

Hum daurenge.

73 Int. STADIUM - Afternoon 73

The stadium is crowded and there are more than 50 participants in the long line behind Gagan.

BABLU

Itna sare log? Pura banaras competition mein daud raha hai ka?

The announcer takes a mike and starts talking.

ANNOUNCER

Suniye-suniye bhaiyon, banaras ke naujawaan khilladion.

Aap log sab ek line banaiye aur dhyaan se suniye. Competition aaj se 19 din ke baad hai.

Kal ek daud pratiyogita hogi purane maidan mein. Aap logo mein se keval 1 ko competition mein daudne ka mauka milega. Jeetne wale ko 11 lakh rupaye ka inaam diya jayega.

BABLU

Matlab samjhe guru?

GAGAN

Kal ke race mein top 20 me rehna hai, tabhi selection hoga.

Bablu fills up a registration form for the race at one of the booths.

Insert of sunset.

74 int. GAGAN'S HOUSE (TERRACE) - Night 74

Gagan is seated silently on the terrace, when his dadaji comes up to him.

GAGAN

Humko bhut darr lagg raha hai daddu itna asaaan nahi hone wala hai kuch bhi.

Dadaji

Pata hai tumko jab tumhara baap tumse bhi chota tha, bhut darta tha humse…

Gagan

Kya baat kar rahe hai aapse darr?

Dadaji

Haan…

(thinking to himself)

Hum sala ghar aate the aur oo...

(laughs a bit)

Humare aane ke awaaz se hi chup jata tha… fir ek din ooo humare paas aaya kehne laga babuji humko na ek naav

chalana hai… hum hairaan… puche kya karega bolta hai etna log aata hai banaras sabko ghumaenge…
Us din uske aankh mein pehle baar darr ki jagah aatam vishwas tha… bol raha pura ghar ka haalaat badal dega… beta pura zindagi guzaar diye hum kya mila humko… tumhare paida hone se pehle tumhar dadi chali gayi…
Akele padd gaye the hum, darr lagta tha ki kaise rahenge… fir tum aaya… chota saa…
(his face brightens up)
Humara sara darr… jhat se khatam ho gaya… uske baad hum samjhe darr jo hai oo bhi pal bhar ka mehmaan hai bas… samjhe babu ab fikar choro aur apna kaam karo.
BLACK OUT:
75 Int. FIELD - Day 75
At the early rays of sunrise, Gagan practices running in a field trying to run as fast as he can. He is quickly exhausted but confident that he can run, and is now mentally prepared for the race.
cut to:
All the participants of the qualifier race are gathered at the start line along with Gagan, meanwhile Gagan completes the race at no. 6.
match cut to:
Gagan runs fast along with multiple participants. With a lot of struggling somehow he manages to get 3rd in this round.
match cut to:
In the third round, Gagan is ahead of everyone which makes him more confident. But in no time the rivals start passing him. He feels his heartbeat getting heavier, yet he manages to reach at the 1st position. Bablu sees Gagan being upset.

COMMENTATOR

Aur ee humlogo mil gaya humare banaras ka winner...... kya dauda hai ee khiladi...

The commentator's voice fades along with the surrounding sounds.

Bablu

Bhai hum tumko bole thhe ke sala pura banaras me tumse tez dhawak hai hi nahi... bas ab final bacha hai usko jeet lo...

Gagan doesn't react and is gasping for breath.

76 Ext. GANGA GHAT - Night 76

Gagan is sitting on his boat all by himself. Feeling tensed. His dad comes from behind and hold his shoulder to comfort him.

Murari Ji

Kya soch rahe ho...

Gagan

Lagta hai humse nahi ho paayega.

Murari Ji

Arre aise kahe bol rahe ho. Try karne se pahle hi haar man rahe ho.

Gagan

Hume training ki zarurat hai papa.

Murari Ji

Ek aadmi hai jo tumhari madat kar sakta hai.

Gagan

Kaun?

Murari Ji

Malkhan...

Gagan

Inka naam to pahle kabhi nahi sune.

Murari Ji

Beta ee joh competition mein tum hissa le rahe ho na ussi competition ka baap tha wo.
Woh bhi ek baar ke liya nahi, Lagataar 6 baar ke liye. Uske seekhaye huye dhavak aaj national international khel rahe hain.
Gagan
Kaha milengey Malkhan?
Murari Ji
Log kehta hai chandauli me rehte hai, yaha se thoda door hai… chalte hai.
They all leave together.
77 Ext. ROAD - Morning 77
QUICK MONTAGE
- Murari ji, Gagan & Bablu are leaving for Chandauli to meet Malkhan in tempo.
- Dialogs between Murariji and Gagan about Malkhan.
78 Int. malkhan HOUSE - Day 78
Murari ji takes Gagan to meet Malkhan (a retired runner) the next day. They see an old man running behind 10 chicken with such energy until he finally grabs it with both hands.
Murari Ji
Pata to yahi ka bataya tha… chalo andar.
Gagan
Ji Namaste.
Malkhan
Namaste, ka kaam hai?
Gagan
Humko malkhan sir se milna hai.
Malkhan
Kahe?
Gagan

Humko unse kaam hai.

Malkhan

Humne usko kaam se nikaal diya.

Gagan

Kaam se nikaal diya matlab?

Malkhan

Matlab retirement… hum hi Malkhan khan hai, bolo kya kaam hai?

Gagan

Daud pratiyogita me humne bhaag liya hai.

Malkhan

Ek kaam karo bhaag lo yahan se.

Gagan

Dekhiye yeh zingadi aur maut ka savaal hai aapko madat karna hi padega

Malkhan

Dekho training dena humne bandh kar diya hai… Sab log yahan ate hain sikh ke chale jaate hain.

Phir antarrashtriya khiladi ban jaate hain aur guru ko bhul jaate hain. Beimaan dhokebaaz log saale!

Gagan

Hum aisa nahi kareingey.

Malkhan

(points towards Bablu)

Iske to mastak me likha hai ke ee chor hai.

Bablu

Pranaam…

Malkhan

Shut up… Haan bhai chaliye.

koi training nahi hogi.

Gagan

Aur koi apna marr raha ho, toh kya karna chahiye?

Malkhan stops.

Gagan

Hamara dost ko cancer hai.. Illaj mein bahut paise kharch hoga aur competition jeetne ke alava mere pass koi aur chaara nahi…

Malkhan takes a sip of alcohol and look into the sky. He is into some thoughts.

Malkhan

Ab emotional kar diya toh hum kya bole…

Hum train karenge lekin humari kuch sharte hain.

Bablu

Hume aapki saari sharte manzur hai.

Malkhan

Abe assi ghat ke rassi kya naam bataya… Bablu Pahle shart to sun lo…

Pahla - Suryodaye se pahle tum hume field me chahiye.

Dusra - Jaisa hum bole waisa karna hoga. Koi kintu-parantu nahi chahiye aur teesra yeh bina tel ka deepak yahan dikhna nahi chahiye…

Sabse mehtvapurn, shaam hoti hai hume ek paua chahiye.

Gagan

Hume aapki saari sharte manjoor hai.

Malkhan

Kal pratah suryodaye hone se pahle maidaan mein.

79 Ext. OLD HOUSE Ground - Day 79

MONTAGE - Song 4 - Motivational:

- Gagan and Malkhan meet early in the morning and start practicing running.
- Gagan runs through the city every morning while passing near Anaya's home. He waits to see a glimpse of her but as soon as Anaya comes to the window, she sees him and goes back in.

- Gagan tries out different exercises under Malkhan's guidance.
- Gagan tries to keep his pace along with Bablu riding a bike. He starts slow but after several tries across days, he is able to keep up with Bablu.
- Gagan has very simple food and meditates. He is now a transformed person.
- Gagan and Bablu visit Mukesh at the Hospital.
- Gagan feels a sudden urge to eat Gutkha.
- Gagan's speed increases gradually and he now runs with a heightened energy, due to the constant training.

MONTAGE ENDS:

80 Int. HOSPITAL (ICU) - Day 80

Bablu is seated near Mukesh when he notices Mukesh trying to tell him something.

Mukesh

(barely speaking)

Bhai humara ek kaam karega?

Bablu

Kaho…

Mukesh

Phone nikal apna.

Bablu takes out his phone and starts the video. Mukesh talks in a weak tone.

Mukesh

Mera naam Mukesh hai.

Bablu cries as Mukesh's voice fades off.

81 Ext. malkhan HOUSE - Evening 81

Gagan is running in the field, but is feeling a bit tired and Malkhan sees Gagan leaves suddenly. Malkhan wonders where he is going.

82 Ext. Village paan shop - Evening 82

Gagan goes jogging to the main road, and stops for a breath. He feels an uncontrollable urge to have Gutkha and runs towards the city of Banaras.

Gagan takes the packet of Gutkha and tears it, bringing it closer to his mouth, but stops suddenly. He looks at the packet for a few moments but then throws it onto the ground.

83 ext. malkhan HOUSE - Evening 83

Gagan puts his head down in shame and walks back slowly towards Malkhan's Home.

On reaching there, he sees Malkhan standing there with a smile on his face. He feels odd as he had expected to be scolded by Malkhan.

Malkhan

Ab aaya tum jeetne ke liye…

As he is about to touch Malkhan's feet, Malkhan hugs him like a father proud of his son.

CUT TO:

84 Ext. GANGA GHAT - Night 84

There is a big crowd at the Ganga ghat celebrating the evening aarti (prayers). A lot of lights and lamps burnt make the place look beautiful.

Gagan reaches there and finds Anaya after some searching. He takes a hold of her hand and brings her aside. He tells her that there is a difference in a mistake and a crime, and that there is no mistake which would cause a relationship to end.

He tells her a lot about how he feels and that if she truly loved him, she would not have left him mid-way like that.

DIALOGS TO BE ADDED.

Anaya

Gagan, tum kar kya rahe ho, choro humara haath…

After having said all that he wanted, he leaves without waiting to hear from Anaya, who looks at him walk away.

85 Int. GAGAN'S HOUSE (VERANDA) - Morning 85

It is finally the day of the competition.

Mukesh's Mother

Humar paas tumko dene ke liye to kuch nahi hai beta, lekin haa ek dua hai maa ka ke bhagwan har maa ko tmhare tarah bacha de…

Mukesh's mother feeds a spoon of curd to Gagan for good luck with a tear in her eye feeling proud about him. Gagan wipes the tears in her eyes.

GAGAN

Aap tension na lo… jeet ke aaenge.

Gagan thanks her, takes her blessings and leaves with Bablu.

86 Int. OLD HOUSE - Day 86

Malkhan excitedly turns on his TV to watch the live telecast of Gagan's race.

87 Int. STADIUM/town - Day 87

Gagan takes his place on the starting line, when he sees Anaya in the audience. She smiles at him and signals all the best to him. This boosts him up even further.

The race starts with a gunshot. The contestants run alongside each other. At the same time Bablu gets a call and leaves.

88 Int. HOSPITAL (ICU) - Day 88

On reaching the hospital Bablu meets the doctor tells him that Mukesh's condition is very serious and that they can't say much about what will happen. He would need to be operated immediately.

DIALOGS TO BE ADDED.

89 Int. STADIUM - Day 89

Sounds of the medical instruments along with a heartbeat are heard as Gagan runs on the ground. He runs faster than before and overtakes his opponents. He is almost near the finish line.

The heartbeat sound turns to that of a flat line as Gagan crosses the finish line. He stumbles and falls down, with a sinking feeling in his heart.

The other participants wish him but he doesn't react.

The sun sets behind Gagan, leaving just a silhouette of him.

blackout:

90 Ext. SHAMSHAAN GHAT - Evening 90

Mukesh's body is burning on a pyre, and his younger brother Chhotu is lighting it up. Mukesh's mother is wailing continuously while Gagan and Bablu are also nearby trying to console her but unable to stop themselves from tears.

Gagan hugs his father with sheer desperation.

THE END

www.ingramcontent.com/pod-product-compliance
Lightning Source LLC
Chambersburg PA
CBHW031353230926
51848CB00002B/498